Too
Close

GAYLE CURTIS

twenty7

First published in Great Britain in 2016 by Twenty7 Books

This paperback edition published in 2016 by
Twenty7 Books
80–81 Wimpole St, London W1G 9RE
www.twenty7books.co.uk

A CIP catalogue record for this book is available from the British Library.

Paperback ISBN: 978-1-7857-7028-9

Also available as an ebook

1 3 5 7 9 10 8 6 4 2

Typeset by IDSUK (Data Connection) Ltd

Printed and bound by Clays Ltd, St Ives Plc

Twenty7 Books is an imprint of Bonnier Zaffre,
a Bonnier Publishing company
www.bonnierzaffre.co.uk
www.bonnierpublishing.co.uk

For my parents, celebrating their 50th wedding anniversary.

To my husband, Christopher, with all my love.

Dedicated to my mother-in-law, Carol Mary Curtis.

PROLOGUE

The green suitcase resting on the purlin swirled around in Cecelia's mind as though it had turned to liquid and was curling its way around a basin towards the plug hole. It moved from one side of her mind to the other as she tried to hold on to it, but it was too late, she'd woken up and the dream was becoming nothing but a blur. She'd dreamt about the green suitcase on the purlin on many occasions but this time it felt different – this vision was clearer somehow, evocative of a distant memory. She knew the suitcase had been her mother's but she'd never discovered what it contained and these thoughts had haunted her ever since.

Waking up now, the dream becoming an unreachable memory as it wisped its way up to the high ceiling and burst on the Victorian cornice, she thought she heard movement coming from the other bedrooms. Climbing from her warm bed she tiptoed down the corridor to peer quietly into the room next to hers, but all was still as she'd expected. The house was motionless and quiet – empty, lacking the vibrancy and warmth it had once held within its walls.

Back in bed, Cecelia drifted off fairly quickly but soon found her mind returning to the green suitcase on the purlin. She was sitting in front of it, legs swinging like a gymnast on a beam. On the other side of the suitcase sat her brother, Sebastian, one leg bent up to his chest and the other swinging in time with hers. He stared at her, leant forward and tipped the case from its wooden rest and that's when she woke again, heart pounding in her chest, sweat forming on her brow. The uneasy feeling continued when she reached for her glass of water on the bedside table and saw her daughter, Caroline, standing by her bed. It was dark, apart from a glimmer from the open window, but she could make out the shape of her tiny frame.

'You startled me. What's the matter?' she said in a loud whisper.

'Come with me, I want to show you something.'

'It's late, go back to bed.' Cecelia pulled back the quilt, preparing to get out of bed so she could march Caroline back to her room.

'I need to show you something first,' Caroline said as she grabbed Cecelia's wrist before she'd even had a chance to stand up.

'You're so cold! How long have you been out of bed?' asked Cecelia. She followed Caroline out of the bedroom and was led to the top of the wide staircase by the small, determined child.

'Cold hands, warm heart,' Caroline whispered to Cecelia.

'Where did you hear that? Come on now, this is silly, get back into bed . . .' It suddenly dawned on Cecelia that Caroline could be sleepwalking – a habit that she seemed to have inherited from

Cecelia – and that she shouldn't really wake her. She pulled her wrist from the child's grip as gently as she possibly could and tried to steer her by the shoulders down the corridor and back to her bedroom, but there was no chance of manoeuvring her anywhere.

'Please, I need to show you this and then I promise I'll sleep.'

Cecelia decided to indulge her daughter, knowing if she did she'd only be minutes away from getting back into her own warm bed.

'Let me find the light switch –'

'No! Don't turn the light on, you won't be able to see it. There's light from the moon shining through the windows.'

She was right, there was just enough illumination to guide them down the stairs but Cecelia couldn't help feeling there was something odd in Caroline's tone of voice and it caused a cold draught to whisper across her skin. She shivered slightly at the sight of the silvery light that was shining across the kitchen floor below, adding to her feeling of unease.

'This is ridiculous; we need to get back to bed.'

A blanket of light suddenly lit the hallway causing Cecelia to squint and look above her. As her eyes began to adjust to the starkness she saw her husband, Samuel, on the landing, looking as bleary-eyed as she was.

'What are you doing?' His voice was a croaky whisper.

'You frightened me,' she laughed nervously, her hand reaching for her throat. 'I think Caroline's sleepwalking again.' She looked down and noticed her daughter had wandered off.

'What?'

'Go back to bed, Samuel. I'll find her and get her tucked up.'

'Cecelia, there's nobody there. Caroline's in bed asleep, I just checked.'

Cecelia halted on the stairs.

'You must have been dreaming,' said Samuel.

'But, she was just here with me . . . I was holding her hand . . . we . . .' She noticed Samuel's hand was on Caroline's bedroom door, which was ajar.

'You must have been sleepwalking. Come back to bed.'

'Caroline's down here, I know she is . . .' Her heart began to thump harder as she spoke the words over and over in her head, the feel of the cold little hand still on her skin.

'Cecelia, there is no one there. Please, sweetheart . . .'

She ran downstairs, flicking all the lights on so she could check in every room. She even went down into the cellar where Caroline rarely ventured because she found it too creepy. The rooms creaked with irritability as if they too had suddenly been disturbed from their sleep. The last place she checked was the garden room and that's where she felt a change in the atmosphere. It was only very slight but it was almost as though there had been some sort of movement in there that had stopped suddenly. She switched the light on and off a few times to see if there was any change. After a few moments she realised how ridiculous she was being – she had just frightened herself. She turned to go back upstairs and let out a piercing scream as she ran straight into Samuel. Cold sweat prickled across her skin as he grabbed her arms and she tried to catch her breath.

'It's just me, silly. You've got yourself into a right state.' He held her tightly and she felt the fear begin to disperse. 'Go back to bed and I'll bring you some tea.'

Cecelia didn't argue with him; she was still shaking and was confused by what had just occurred. She went up the uneven staircase and into Caroline's bedroom, pausing for a minute before returning to her own bed. Her daughter was fast asleep, entangled in the bedclothes. It did nothing to settle Cecelia's turbulent mind though – she still felt uneasy. Maybe Samuel was right and she had been sleepwalking. But she wasn't convinced and she could still feel the tiny hand she'd thought was Caroline's in hers, her quiet whispering voice in the memory of her mind.

Hearing the kettle boil she went back to bed and waited for Samuel. They exchanged very few words and eventually he cradled her in his arms as he always did when she'd had a nightmare. She was glad of the comfort but as soon as she heard his deep level breathing she got up and went to sit in Caroline's room, wanting to be near her. The words, 'cold hands, warm heart' repeated in her head until they became something quite different – 'cold hands, cold heart'.

PART 1

1

1984

The dent in the veneered table was where Cecelia kept most of her thoughts. She often wondered where they all went as she rubbed the dark lacquered chink of wood. The veneer had been missing for so long on that tiny splinter, it was almost as though it had always been like that. But, of course, it hadn't. She had a vague idea how it had come to be in the first place, some broken crockery and jagged words. But she was fascinated by the way the pale lined, checked pattern had been interrupted and she liked to rub at this spot when she was thinking. It very often brought back memories of other times she'd sat at the table in the echoic kitchen. Radio Two would be playing in the background as she did her homework whilst her mother, Yvonne, cooked the family dinner. It would be warm, bright and filled with the smell of food, which always made her feel homely in the big cold house with just her twin brother, Sebastian, and their mother. The best of times was when it was just the three of them. The thought of her mother landed like a heavy stone in the sandy pit of her stomach.

Today was different. Today she sat at the table opposite Sebastian.

There were no lights on, or food smells to arouse their senses and no Radio Two tinkling in the background. The Aga was ghostly, having not been stoked up, and was a shadow of its normal robustness as it tried to push out a minimal amount of heat. Cecelia could hear the wind swirling down the chimney and whooshing into the flue. Without their mother there, everything was grey. The house was always like that when she was gone and it reminded her of the magic colouring books she'd had a few years ago, the kind you painted with water to make the colours appear. That's how she saw her mother, the magic liquid to colour her dim grey world. But today there was a heavy melancholic mist swirling with the wind outside and through the cracks of the windows and the mortar between the bricks and into the house. She'd known this day would come, although she'd hoped it wouldn't.

'She's left us,' Sebastian blurted across the table.

Cecelia paused in rubbing the veneer and watched his words skid towards her.

'Shut up. She hasn't left.'

'Where is she then?'

'I don't know, probably just held up somewhere . . .'

'I know she's gone because Roger told me. She's not coming back.' He leant forward, resting his arms on the table, interlinking his fingers, first one way, then the other. He was nervous, hiding something – she could tell.

Cecelia stared at him for a few moments but didn't answer. The dark marks under his eyes told her he was feeling a lot more hurt than he was letting on. She could tell that he also knew what had really happened to their mother. She continued rubbing the nick in the veneer and concentrated on wishing that their father, Roger, was the one who was dead instead.

Cecelia and Sebastian were close, although they bickered most of the time and sometimes Cecelia was loath to remember the bond they shared, especially on days like this. They had been one once and now they were two and, although their characters appeared to be different, deep down they were quite the same. Her little mice, their mother called them.

The trouble was she knew he was right about one thing and her irritability was laced with defensiveness. She knew it, as she sat with her brother, waiting for Roger to come in and talk to them both. Their mother wasn't coming back. Not because she'd walked out and left them, but because she was dead. She knew it like she knew she had to go to bed at seven thirty on a school night, had PE and maths on Thursdays and only had fish for dinner on Mondays.

Getting up from her chair, the words Sebastian had blurted out fell from her lap like crumbs.

Sebastian stopped the continuous movement of his fingers. 'Where are you going? Roger said we had to wait here.'

'I'm going upstairs.'

'You'll just make him angry if you leave,' he said, making her want to pinch the back of his arm. 'Stay. Please, Cece.'

Ignoring him she pulled open the kitchen door which led to the hall, hesitating briefly as a blast of cold, musty air hit her full in the face. She shivered and took the steps two at a time.

It was so cold in the rest of the house that when she ran her hand along the Anaglypta-covered walls, they felt wet. She walked the long corridor to her bedroom imagining, as she always did, the green-leafed swirling carpet engulfing her through the floorboards. She didn't go into her parents' bedroom to check if her mother was there; she knew she wasn't. And even though she knew she was dead, she was also quite sure that her side of the wardrobe would be empty. Roger would have made sure it looked like Yvonne had left again.

Once she'd escaped the carpet river Cecelia opened the door to her bedroom, the only place in the house she was allowed some colour. The walls were now plastered with posters of Duran Duran, A-Ha and Tears for Fears, her favourite bands. Sometimes, if she squeezed her eyes shut hard enough she could imagine she was in another house, far away from the fens. She had dreamt once that she lived in a huge modern house, like the ones her school friends resided in on newly built estates. Well-heated and dry with proper rectangular, fenced-in gardens, the local town within walking distance so she could have a social life like everyone else. Then she'd woken up, looked out of the window across the flat patchwork quilt that made up their fields, part of their farmland – which fed and clothed them as Roger liked so often to remind them – and had felt sad for the rest of the day.

A sticky, warm layer of fear rested in the pit of her stomach, as the enormity of what had happened began to reveal itself as a reality. Even though she had Sebastian, she couldn't help feeling she was alone somehow. Something her mother had promised would never happen.

She stood for a minute looking at the pretty, soft green bedroom, with its white melamine furniture – ghosts from the past, reminders from her childhood. This had always comforted her before, but things weren't the same anymore. The intricate gold filigree around the handles and doors seemed dull and lacklustre. The tiny embroidered rose buds that littered the duvet cover appeared to have wilted. And the fluffy cream carpet was flat and unappealing; all of it felt sad and lifeless, unable to cheer her as it once had.

To the left side of her bedroom next to the window was a tiny door leading to a loft space that her father always forbade them to go into. But regardless of his stern lectures, she would often go in there and balance on the purlin, using the beams for support, and Sebastian would join her. It was mainly when their parents were arguing, which was most of the time. It was dark but always warmer than the rest of the house because it was above the kitchen, which had been added to the house in the fifties. As dark and dusty as it was, Cecelia felt safe and comfortable in there. She would sometimes take a cushion and book with her, and balance on the purlin like a gymnast on a beam; one leg stretched out, the other swinging. Roger had recently painted the door shut, more out of a desire for them to obey him than worry that it was dangerous for them to go in there. Bored with their defiance, he had pretended the wood needed protecting but Cecelia had known it was to stop them going through the door.

Unbeknown to Roger, on a particularly bad day of arguments, Cecelia had found her confiscated penknife and chiselled the door open. He'd not caught them in there yet.

Yanking open the stiff door, the smell of gloss still present in the cold draught where the paint had leaked through the cracks, she crawled inside the dark space. Pulling herself along the purlin, she balanced carefully as she drew one leg up to her chest, leaving the other to dangle in mid-air. Rolling up her school trouser leg she rested her mouth on her knee. Her smooth skin cooled her lips, her hard bone making her feel solid once again. She waited for some time, listening to the birds tweeting and scrabbling on the roof. She shivered – the loft space wasn't as warm as it normally was because the Aga down below in the kitchen hadn't been stoked. The damp, musty smell of the loft was prominent today without the usual cooking smells to mask it. Sometimes, when Roger was busy on the farm, Sebastian would hide in the loft with her. They'd take in freshly baked biscuits or pieces of cake straight from the oven and would sit chatting for hours. Sometimes their mother would creep in and tell them ghost stories, the excitement of knowing they shouldn't be in there making it all the more thrilling. These memories – never to be repeated – pained her now.

Thoughts of her mother caused tears to sting Cecelia's eyes, but her mind ran them like a projector she couldn't switch off. She bent forward, pulling her knee closer to her chest, trying to crush the images. They would no longer play board games before bed or watch films together. Then she thought about her and Sebastian's fifteenth birthdays, which were in two months' time.

Yvonne had promised she wouldn't miss their special day. She wouldn't let anything happen that would mean they couldn't be together, however bad it was. It had only been recently she'd told Cecelia that if she was to leave, they would be going with her. Cecelia had made her promise, an oath she knew Yvonne would never break, but now everything had changed.

The door to the kitchen slammed downstairs, vibrating the wooden structure Cecelia was perched on. Her father was home. Listening to the drone of his voice she gathered he was asking Sebastian where she was. Quickly, she slid back along the purlin, practice having made her nimble and, once she'd reached the door, she carefully turned herself round and climbed through the hole. Shutting the door tight behind her, she sat on the bed waiting for him to come up the stairs and into her room, her sore heart pounding in her chest. There was no way she was going downstairs to listen to the rehearsed words about how their mother didn't want to be a part of the family anymore and had left them for a new life. Cecelia knew they weren't true.

After quite some time waiting for Roger to appear, she took her shoes off, got under the blankets and cried herself to sleep.

Disorientated, she awoke to her bedside lamp being switched on and at first, through the haze of sleep, she expected to see Yvonne standing there, forgetting the events of earlier. To her great disappointment it was Roger. Her eyes were slightly sticky from crying and it took her a while to focus.

'I'm prepared to ignore the fact you disobeyed me. What with Yvonne leaving us. Again.' He paused for emphasis as he always did, looking at her, prompting her to go along with his lies. 'Look at me, Cece. Are you listening? There'll be no dinner tonight, understand?'

Cecelia nodded in agreement, knowing this was mainly because her mother wasn't around to cook anything so it suited him to starve them. She wasn't hungry anyway and she was tired. Too tired to correct him and too tired to care about food – it was the least of her worries. There was a tiny spark in her mind telling her to shout at him, tell him she hated him, but she had become mute, something which often happened to Cecelia when she was upset. But she did hate him. She hated him for insisting they call their mother Yvonne – because in his mind, 'children who had reached double figures were too old to address their parents with infantile names'. Cecelia had no problem calling her father Roger but never referred to her mother as anything other than mother. She hated Roger as much as she loved Yvonne.

She stared at him now, more hatred pricking at her skin as he lectured her about what a disappointment she was and how he didn't want 'his girl' going down the wrong path.

He leaned towards her face and touched her cheek but she flinched and turned away. 'We both know what happened. If you hadn't interfered, your mother would be here now. I don't have a licence for that gun, so keep your bloody mouth shut,' he hissed. 'Just do what I tell you and no one will get into any trouble.'

She couldn't bear to look at his large, bald shiny forehead decorated with sweaty wisps of blond hair, the colour of which she'd inherited from him. His long nose and elongated face were his and his alone. She and Sebastian had inherited his dark blue eyes and hair colour but their soft, small features belonged to their mother.

Leaning further forward he attempted to kiss her goodnight, something he didn't normally do, and she recoiled, wondering why he always smelt ever so slightly greasy. It made her feel sick and she tried to push the suffocating sensation away. As so often happened when Cecelia's voice failed her, she lashed out physically and caught her father in the face with her tightly screwed up hands. He restrained her immediately, pinning both her skinny wrists above her head with one of his giant hands. With his other hand he covered her mouth, making it hard for her to breathe. He pressed her head into the pillow, hurting her lips and teeth and then released her as if nothing had happened.

'Don't forget to read that letter . . . it's important you move on from this as quickly as possible. Accept what I've told you; it'll be easier for you to come to terms with, easier than pining for someone you can't have. She's not coming back this time. My mother was the same. I can still remember her walking out of this very house and not even turning back when she got to the gate.'

Trying to get away from you, Cecelia thought, but didn't, couldn't say. She concentrated on her chipped nail varnish, pretending she didn't care, desperate for him to leave. She couldn't believe he was trying to force feed her these lies, convincing himself it was the truth, when they both knew exactly what had happened that day.

'I've put it on your bedside table. Your brother has read his.'

Puzzled, she sat up and looked around.

Once Roger had gone she peered at the letter he'd left propped up against her night light. She'd ignored much of what he'd said and only vaguely remembered him mentioning it was from their mother.

She picked up the small brown envelope and read the typing on the front. It said simply Cecelia. She turned it over to see what was on the other side but there was nothing there other than an over-licked seal which was obviously Roger's handiwork.

Opening the tiny drawer to her bedside table she placed the unopened letter inside. She wasn't going to read something she knew to be a lie. She knew her mother couldn't have written this letter. She reached underneath postcards, beads and hair bands until she found the small soapstone hippo her mother had bought her for winning a medal at gymnastics club. In one of her many tempers, Cecelia had picked it up and thrown it at the wall, breaking its elongated snout. She could still see the crack where Yvonne had glued it back together. There were minute chips of it missing but she still loved it even though it was damaged.

Bizarrely, Roger had punished her that day for contradicting him and not Sebastian for putting his fist through a pane of glass on the utility door when Cecelia had shut him out. In a temper she'd broken one of her favourite things, regretting it later. There were a lot of moments she regretted.

She'd been made to stand with no shoes or socks on in one of the old World War Two hangars that were situated in the farmyard. However much Yvonne protested, Roger would always have his own way. He'd repeat over and over about what his father had done to him and how it had made him the man he was today. On better days, Cecelia and Sebastian would mimic him behind his back, desperately gulping down laughter in case they were caught.

She hated this particular punishment the most: pitch dark, bitterly cold and filled with eerie whisperings from people past. These were Roger's winter recriminations, the cold being the core of the pain. The summer ones, Cecelia found easier, although they had become more traumatic, but she knew he wouldn't do anything that he could possibly be caught for. His latest reprisal had been making her sit on an old stool in the field while he fired his .22 rifle at rabbits behind her, laughing each time she flinched. Skinning and gutting the rabbits would follow but she'd grown used to this, hardened to farm life.

But the winter punishments involved physical pain. Sebastian would meet Cecelia in her bedroom afterwards and hold her tightly to warm her up while she cried, knowing himself how bad the punishments were. Occasionally they would be punished at the same time – it never felt as bad when Sebastian was by her side – but in the main Cecelia was alone. Her mother would then stand her in the bath tub, pretending everything was normal, as she ran tepid water to try and gradually warm Cecelia's feet and legs which would be covered in purple and orange blotches. Then slowly, so she didn't get chilblains, Yvonne would add more and more hot water. The relief was both painful and comforting. She never got used to these kinds of punishments and always cried, which upset her mother even more.

Closing the drawer, determined not to open the letter from Roger, Cecelia got a small amount of comfort from secretly defying him, even in this small way. She'd just let him think she'd accepted his version of events but she knew he'd written two letters, one to her and the other to Sebastian, pretending to be their mother. It wouldn't have surprised her if he'd written one to himself to make it look even more convincing. Yvonne had never had much need to address anything to them in a letter unless they went to stay with family or friends during the summer holidays. But Cecelia remembered very well that her and Sebastian's birthday cards were always addressed *to my darling* or *my sweetheart*. Whereas the front of this envelope just read, *Cecelia*. And Yvonne never used a typewriter – everything was always hand written. Anyone who knew her and saw the letters would know they hadn't been written by her.

Opening the drawer and picking up the letter again, Cecelia hesitated, considering whether or not to read it. The sinking feeling of knowing the truth poured into her stomach and defiance prevailing, she put the letter back into the drawer. Her previous determination strengthened like drying concrete and she picked up the soapstone hippo, rubbing its smooth side for comfort. It was the only tiny bit of control she had over her father, as minute as it was, and she didn't want to open the letter and ruin that. She wouldn't give him the satisfaction of knowing her eyes had read over his pretend words.

Standing the hippo on her table, she turned out the lamp and lay there in the stark silence. Her mind quickly drifted to the previous night when she'd been lying there with her head on her mother's chest, listening to a story from when she had been a teenager. Yvonne had just had a bath and sweat from the hot water still ran down her chest and the agate pendant she never took off was covered in steam. It was the necklace that Cecelia had always held as a child when her mother was telling her a story, a comfort, a stamp that was so familiar it represented Yvonne in all her completeness. It had fascinated Cecelia for as long as she could remember; one half of the stone was mottled dark green with a small portion of it striped pale sea-blue.

It had also been the previous night when Yvonne had told Cecelia she'd been saving some money and almost had enough for them all to leave White Horse Farm and to get away from Roger. Cecelia had told Sebastian later that night, when he'd sat on her bed before lights out, but he told her, as he always did, that Yvonne was just trying to appease her, to cover the guilt she felt for staying. But the words contained conviction, something she hadn't heard from her mother before and she held on to them. Those empty words had made her angry the following day, nasty spiteful letters that had snapped and bitten at her ankles.

2

Sebastian read the letter his father had given him – a minimal amount of words on some notepaper. He folded it once, twice, turned it in his fingers and repeated the process until he couldn't continue anymore. Then he squeezed the tiny lump of compressed paper in-between his thumb and middle finger, the events from earlier that day stuffed between every crease. Passing it to his left hand he repeated the ritual, squeezing it with what he deemed to be the same level of strength. Enough to ease the anxiety within him that always rose when he felt something wasn't equal and balanced out in the way he wanted.

Pictures from earlier that day flickered across his vision like a projector film, each time becoming increasingly jumbled. He couldn't remember who he'd seen with the gun first, his mother or his father. Roger's words penetrated his head, fading any memories he had about what he'd seen. It was irrelevant now. Somehow he'd managed to tell Cecelia what Roger had told him to repeat over and over again: Yvonne has left, she's not coming back.

Sebastian couldn't tell her the truth; she wouldn't be able to hide it and they would most definitely be put into foster care and separated if anyone found out. If he'd gone to school as normal that day instead of staying behind to help Roger on the farm, he wouldn't have known anything about it. Sounds that he could still hear clearly now echoed in his ears. Noises that had brought him running into the house and into the kitchen. Roger had come up behind him and gently placed his large hands over his eyes and mouth, carefully removing him from the room. The last thing he'd seen was his mother's legs and feet from under the kitchen table. For a split second he'd had a comical moment where it had reminded him of the scene from *The Wizard of Oz*, and as Roger tried to erase the memories from his mind with his soothing words it was as if his mother's feet began to wilt and shrivel away. You didn't see anything, you didn't see anything, you didn't see anything, his father whispered into his ear over and over again. All he found himself thinking about as he shook with fear in his father's arms was the ridiculous observation that his mother's legs weren't lying at a level angle to the table. He wanted desperately to go in there and move her – his anxiety, the draught he called it, had risen in his gut, swirling like the wind coming across the fields. He'd experienced this strange sensation the first time his father had punished him for something he hadn't done. He was so indignant about the entire episode, so overwhelmed with angry tears that he thought his temper would rise out of his mouth and swallow him whole.

Before Sebastian could do anything, Roger ordered him upstairs to get changed for school and fetch his school bag, before sending him on his way, telling him all the time to act normally and that things weren't what they looked like. Upon his return, earlier than Cecelia because she had detention, Roger had told him the story he was to tell her later, pretending that Sebastian hadn't seen anything.

There was one thing Roger couldn't erase and that was the foreboding atmosphere that had settled over the farmhouse during the course of the day; a cold and empty, almost tangible air had descended and Sebastian felt more unsteady than he ever had in all his years. Unsure. Unsafe. Yvonne had more of a presence on the farm than Sebastian had realised.

Checking the gun cabinet again on his way to the kitchen, Sebastian looked behind him, Roger's words so clear in his mind. If anyone asks about the gunshot noises, we were shooting rabbits, the stern words Roger had spat at him upon his return from school still marked on his face.

Placing the kettle on the stove, he tentatively sat on one of the kitchen chairs and stared at the space where his mother had been lying. So easily he could let go, the sickness in his chest threatening to bubble over into his throat, spewing the truth onto the floor. He couldn't do it, couldn't do this, whatever it was they were going to do. Carry on as normal he supposed. That wasn't going to work but he also knew that if Roger sensed any defiance, neither he nor Cecelia would get away from the farm alive.

He picked up an old cloth hanging on the back of the chair and began to wipe at a dark spot that was bothering him on the Aga. He pushed harder, wondering if it had been there before; whatever it was had been baked on by the heat from earlier that day. The stain became the focus of his concentration as he ferociously rubbed it, equally with his left hand as well as his right, keeping the balance, maintaining the nature of his symmetry. He was trying to erase the pictures in his head but it made little difference to the way he felt.

The whistling of the kettle brought Sebastian back into the room, to the place he didn't want to be.

3

The following night, Cecelia scoffed down the slices of buttered malt loaf Sebastian had brought her. She'd been sleepwalking since she was small but it was the first time in almost a year. If Sebastian heard her moving about in the night, he would get up and quietly follow, keeping her safe until she eventually woke up. She would shake afterwards, desperately needing food to raise her sugar levels, the exertion of energy making her hungry. A doctor had once told her parents that the involuntary muteness could possibly originate from her sleepwalking episodes; dreams so vivid they rendered her speechless. She always knew she was having nightmares but could never recall the details. Roger thought it was a load of old rubbish and continually voiced the opinion that she was able to talk when she felt like it and was just attention seeking.

'I thought you were heading across the fields when you stepped outside the back door,' Sebastian said, rubbing Cecelia's legs as he tried to warm her. 'I never thought you'd go into the old grain store.'

Cecelia shrugged, her silence still blanketing her voice. She didn't even try to speak – she knew when her voice was there and when it wasn't, although she could never explain why.

They were perched on some old bales of straw, a large torch propped on top of some old machinery to give them light. There were very few punishments endured in the grain store and they both quite liked it there as it seemed to have a different atmosphere to the rest of the farm. Cecelia was fascinated by the huge grain mountain in the middle and always had an urge to dive into the centre of it, which made Sebastian laugh. Of course, they never touched the grain; the punishment for doing so wouldn't be worth it.

'I wondered if your nightmare might have jolted your voice into action, like it would have the opposite effect for a change, seeing as you were already mute?'

Cecelia shook her head and listened to him talking gently, as he always did when she'd been sleepwalking – it soothed the panic she often felt afterwards.

Looking at his face in the half-light she noticed how much he'd changed in the last few weeks – there was a maturity appearing and she'd only just become aware of it. She thought she'd die without him, even more so now in their current circumstances. Being close to Yvonne was one thing but her relationship with her twin brother was something else altogether. They shared so much, a lot more than other siblings, and had done since they were born. Yvonne would often tell them how they could never be apart, not for a moment, and if they were one or the other would start screaming. Their bond had grown even more over the years and she knew it was forever, no matter what happened.

'You must have been dreaming about this place to walk all the way across the yard, past the hangar. Why don't you try going to sleep thinking about somewhere really nice, far away, and I'll follow you there?' It was supposed to be a joke but the childish tone made it sound so sad Cecelia reached across and clasped Sebastian's hand, reassuring him with her eyes.

'I know it will be OK, we've got each other, right?' Sebastian said, squeezing her hand in return. Cecelia felt the usual warm tendrils curl up from her stomach, reaching to her heart. They were feelings she was aware might not be normal for a brother and sister to have.

Breaking the moment, Cecelia pulled his fingers to her mouth and kissed them hard, letting him know how much he meant to her, how loved he was, despite all that had happened.

4

There was something in the kisses Cecelia planted on Sebastian's fingers, a knowing, a guilt almost; as though she was stamping words into his hand that she couldn't say, even if she had been able to speak. It was a strange feeling, so odd because she'd never kept anything from him before as far as he was aware. He began to wonder if she knew what he was hiding, what he'd seen on the farm the previous day, but he couldn't work out how she could possibly know.

'Is everything all right, Mouse?'

Cecelia nodded and put her finger to her lips. She was staring past him, towards the door, her hearing far more acute than his – possibly heightened as she'd lost her voice. A couple of seconds later the noise of the large door scraping on the concrete startled them. Roger stood there with a rifle in his hand. It always amazed Sebastian how quiet he was when he wanted to be, lurking everywhere, unseen most of the time.

'What's going on in here?'

'Cecelia was sleepwalking. I followed her to make sure she was all right.' Sebastian immediately dashed to his sister's defence.

'I don't need you to talk for her. She can tell me herself.' Roger stepped closer to Cecelia, his face distorted in the dawn light from outside and the torch, which was shining away from him.

Sebastian looked at the rifle and then at Cecelia as she opened and closed her mouth, the words evaporating in her throat.

'I heard talking in here, so I know she can speak. Come on, what have you got to say for yourself?'

'It was me, I was talking, not Cece.'

'Shut up, boy. I know what I heard.' Roger turned the rifle he was holding, nudging Cecelia's legs with the butt. 'Come on, speak up.'

Sebastian wanted to grab his father but memories of his mother laying under the kitchen table snapped into his mind, leaving him fearful of what Roger might do to them both. The twins had always been able to gauge his moods, know his limits. However bad things were, there was an imaginary line Roger would never cross, or so they had thought until yesterday.

This moment, right now, was turning nasty and he had no way of knowing how to diffuse it. Cecelia was helpless and her silence was making matters worse and he knew that soon she'd get angry and things would escalate.

'I can't hear you!' Roger said, almost lyrically, as he shoved Cecelia again, causing her to pull her knees up, tucking herself into a ball.

'Only talking when you feel like it? Sleepwalking? Bollocks! You got away with it before, when Yvonne was here, but not now. If you don't speak up, I'll send you and your brother straight into those fields and you can spend the day potato riddling.'

Sebastian looked at Cecelia and she at him as they waited for the punishment to unfold.

'In the cold . . . until you've finished . . . in your night clothes . . . if it takes you until tomorrow, so be it.'

There was a shake, a weakness in Roger's voice that Sebastian knew Cecelia had detected too. This was a minor punishment compared to what they normally had to suffer. Most of the fields had been harvested by the labourers employed on the farm and they knew that between them it wouldn't take long to finish the small field that was left. If it meant a day off school to spend with each other, Sebastian didn't care.

'Just because your mother's not here, don't think I'm going to be lenient with either of you.' Roger stepped closer to Cecelia, pushing his face into hers. Sebastian held his breath – he knew what was coming, a last attempt to force some noise from his sister.

Roger grabbed Cecelia's hair and pulled her head back. She opened her mouth but still no sound escaped. Sebastian stood up, getting ready to defend his sister before her temper got the better of her, but her eyes were now pools of water and she put up her hand, signalling him not to. If they were to get away with no punishment other than potato riddling for the day, this time they needed to let Roger finish asserting the power he thought he had over them.

One day, Sebastian thought to himself, he would find an opportunity to take that rifle his father was so attached to and blast him across the farm with it. He would never let anyone else touch his Cecelia, not ever.

5

About a week later, Cecelia arrived home from school to find Roger sitting at the table with two women she didn't recognise.

'Here's my girl!' He beckoned her over with his long arms as though she was five years old, and she reluctantly moved towards him, slinging her bag on the floor, trying to be casual but frantically going over Roger's words in her head.

'Say hello, Cecelia. These ladies are from social services. They've come to see how you and your brother are.' He squeezed her tightly, willing her to speak, to be OK, as he always did in front of visitors.

Both ladies smiled, waiting for Cecelia's response.

'Don't be rude, Cecelia. Say hello.'

There was silence. Even if Cecelia had wanted to speak, she still couldn't. She had never been mute for this length of time before and it was as though someone had crept into her room the first night her mother had disappeared and stolen her voice box.

The awkward silence ensued as Roger squeezed Cecelia even harder, willing her to behave, begging her with his presence to say something. At one point, Cecelia thought he was going to pull her onto his lap – he always acted weird in front of strangers. He was weird, she thought to herself.

'Cat's got her tongue since Yvonne left. Trauma of it, I should expect.' Roger winked, adding conviction to what he was saying.

The two women nodded as they made more notes. Roger began to ramble nervously, filling the space where he'd wanted Cecelia to speak. She stared at the table and watched the little words wander aimlessly around. Some of them slid into the split in the veneer and settled there ready for her to ponder later.

A sharp pinch on the side of her arm brought her back into the room. Roger thought he was safe to administer a little pain to his mute daughter, but her flinch hadn't gone unnoticed by one of the women.

'Have you taken Cecelia or Sebastian to see their GP since all this happened?'

'I didn't see the need . . . They've got me and who knows, she might come back. There's no telling with Yvonne.'

'So, she's done this before?' The woman who noticed Cecelia flinch spoke up for the first time.

'Oh yes, many times. We never know when she might go off on one of her jaunts, do we, Cecelia?' Roger attempted to tickle her, a false smile wavering on his lips.

Cecelia turned to look at him, astounded at the lies dripping from his mouth like warm grease. They slid down his sweaty, dirt-stained shirt and landed on the kitchen floor with a plop. Their mother had only left a couple of times before and it was never for long, but Cecelia's mouth just opened and closed like a small fish gasping for oxygen. It was probably better that she couldn't speak.

Their reactions were observed, causing another awkward silence to descend on the small group. Movement from the corner of Cecelia's eye caused her to look up from the table. It was Sebastian looking at them all through the glass in the door. Ever so briefly, she caught a glimpse of what she thought was hope in his face as he looked at first one woman and then the other. She knew he'd thought one of them was their mother and a heavy sadness pulled at her shoulders as she remembered what happened that day last week. It was the first secret she'd ever kept from her brother.

For all his complaining about how depressing their mother was, she knew most of it was to keep Roger happy. Sebastian adored Yvonne, but tried to keep Roger placid so that neither he nor Cecelia would suffer as much. Roger was very up and down with Sebastian – sometimes he'd love him, but other times he'd hate him – but Sebastian just went along with the moods.

Roger had tried to instigate the same see-saw relationship with Cecelia, but she never treated him any differently, whatever his mood. He'd gradually relented in his game of picking her up and discarding her, knowing she wouldn't submit like her brother. Sebastian often reminded Cecelia of the farm dogs, desperate to please Roger however badly they were treated. His sycophantic ways made her feel quite nauseous as she knew how he really felt. Cecelia always found it difficult to control her temper and would lash out at her father; for every slap he inflicted, she gave him one back until he restrained her.

'Who are they?' Sebastian nodded towards the two women as he walked in and dropped his school bag on the floor beside Cecelia's.

Roger chuckled nervously. 'Don't be rude, Sebastian. They're from social services. They've come to see what's going on with Yvonne . . . your mother. Nothing to worry about, son.'

The two women were visibly baffled at the reference to the twins' mother by her Christian name but Roger had only noticed enough to correct himself.

'We're all right with our dad, aren't we, Mouse?' Sebastian looked at Cecelia pointedly, pleading with her to agree.

Cecelia stood frozen to the spot, unable to speak but knowing if she didn't make some positive gesture towards the women, there would be a backlash after they'd gone. She nodded enthusiastically, her heart tugging at her to stop. Being taken away could mean being separated from Sebastian, and neither of them wanted that, however bad everything was at home.

'Well, I think we have enough information to be going on with now. We'll call back in a few weeks.'

There was a brief silence as Roger started to speak, but then thought better of it.

'You know where we are, you can come anytime . . . Can I ask who sent you? What I mean is, how did you know Yvonne had left?'

'Somebody from the school told us,' one of the women sternly replied. 'But we aren't at liberty to reveal who.'

They thanked Roger and left. Cecelia had followed them to the door, hovering, willing herself to speak so she could reassure them that everything was normal but nothing came out and nobody noticed her struggle except Sebastian.

As soon as they were out of the door, Roger grabbed Cecelia by the back of her arm and pinched her skin so hard she winced, tears immediately springing to her eyes as she tried to pull herself free from his grip. She begged herself not to retaliate. Roger relied on Cecelia losing her temper to justify his punishments.

'Been tittle-tattling to the teachers again! You're such a little bitch, just like your mother!'

Cecelia opened her mouth to speak but nothing came out.

'She didn't, Dad . . . Roger, she can't speak . . .'

Roger held up his hand to silence Sebastian, pulled out a kitchen chair and sat down. Cecelia desperately needed the toilet but she was too scared to move.

'What's all this about, Cece? Did you tell one of the teachers something at school?' His voice was calm, overly nice, patronising and she knew she was in trouble. She opened her mouth to defend herself but still there was no sound. Her eyes were stinging with tears and she was desperately willing herself not to cry because she knew that would be followed by her wetting herself, a childish act for someone of her age, but something she'd not been able to grow out of with the fear that Roger instilled in her.

'You need to tell me what happened or I'm going to have to issue you with a punishment. I know it's been difficult with everything that's happened with Yvonne but you can't be allowed to get away with this behaviour, Cecelia.'

'I did it, Roger. One of the teachers asked if Mum could make it to parents' evening and I told them she'd left . . .' Sebastian was stammering, making the lie obvious. 'Just like you told us to if anyone asked.'

Cecelia glared at Sebastian, tears now tipping over the rims of her eyes. She wanted to shout out, protect her brother but she knew her muteness was still blanketing her.

'Have you been talking at school?'

Cecelia nodded her head. She wasn't going to see Sebastian suffer – it pained her more than her own suffering and his punishments were worse because he was a boy. Before she realised what she was doing, defiance and anger caused her foot to come out and she kicked her father straight in the shin. She bit her bottom lip and stared him square in the face. He barely moved at the impact.

'What did you do that for?!' Sebastian shouted at her.

'Come with me.' Roger held out his hand for her to take.

She stood still, fixed to the spot. She was suddenly hit with the realisation that this time her mother wasn't there to defend her or to offer some sort of comfort later on and it was all her fault. Fear stuck like glue to the bottoms of her feet. The care her mother had always given her after Roger's punishments had been something to focus on while she endured whatever he lined up for her. Sebastian wouldn't be allowed anywhere near her after a punishment without Yvonne around. The thought caused an empty, icy coldness to seep through the pores of her skin.

Sebastian was watching as Roger stared at Cecelia. She fixed her eyes on the floor, not wanting to see her brother's look of despair. A warm sensation began to make its way down the tops of her legs, then she heard the slight trickle of water from her tights onto the unforgiving linoleum-covered floor, cutting through the silence in the stark room.

She looked up to see Roger's expression turn to repulsion. The stillness of the room was suddenly fast-forwarded and Cecelia was grabbed by the arm and dragged through the back door and out into the cold, damp, dusky October night.

'No!' Sebastian ran forward and grabbed his father's arm but Roger shook him off.

'Don't get involved, boy, you know what will happen.'

Cecelia tripped over the steps as he pulled her after him, scuffing her new shoes. She couldn't help thinking how disappointed her mother would be. And then she remembered and the thought sent a jolt through her insides.

The wetness on her tights had already turned cold and her skin pricked with goosebumps as the frosty late afternoon air hit her. She was tearful and exhausted and the thought of having to endure this punishment without her mother was all too much to bear. She sobbed and stumbled as Roger pulled her along, striding forcefully across the yard, his lengthy steps too large for her little frame. She opened her mouth to speak but nothing came out.

The large hangar loomed up ahead. She could hear the doors scraping across the concrete before they'd even been opened, the echoic sound trapped in her memory. In her panic she tried to turn her head and bite Roger's arm but this just caused him to stop mid-stride and shake her like a dog with a rabbit.

She caught her breath when he dragged her beyond the barn and towards the fields. The wind howled across the farm and

Cecelia's heart sunk even lower in her chest, feeling as though it might disappear altogether.

She tried to twist her arm free from his tight grip but he only squeezed harder. They reached the edge of the field near to the first ditch and he swung her round to face him. It was almost dark and she could barely see him. He looked like the cloaked figure she always saw in her dreams. Tears streamed down her chapped face as she begged him with her eyes not to punish her.

'You are disgusting. Take your shoes off and hand them to me.'

Cecelia tried to catch her breath and calm down; she'd cried so much she was gasping. Bile reached her throat and she desperately tried to swallow it, knowing her punishment would be even greater if she was sick as well.

'Come on. Don't make a fuss, just do it.'

Bending forward she took off her shoes, making sure she undid each one instead of slipping them off as she usually did when he wasn't watching.

'Get in.' Roger pushed her towards the ditch.

Cecelia stared at the narrow dyke that was filled with silty orange water, the wind whipping her hair and stinging her eyes.

'You chose your punishment, Cecelia. You want to be dirty and wet then you can stand in the ditch until I tell you to get out.'

It was dark, she hated the dark and even though she despised Roger, she desperately wanted to beg him not to leave her there alone. Yvonne wouldn't have allowed this – the hangar, yes, but not this. She at least had had some influence over Roger, however small.

Defeated, she moved towards the narrow ditch and crouched down to the ground, not quite sure of how she would get in. Although it was deep, the water thankfully looked shallow.

She felt a thump on her side and for a few moments it was as though someone had turned the world upside down, as she fell into the muddy pit. She stood up unsteadily, realising Roger had kicked her in.

'Head up, back straight. I'll come and get you when I think you're ready.'

Cecelia stood up, shakily. With gritted teeth she felt her fists clenching and unclenching by her sides, as though they didn't belong to her.

The dull ache caused by the cold water had started immediately and was gradually making its way up her calves. She opened her mouth to speak but the small cavern was empty and still. Her heart pounded as she moved her feet slowly up and down in the shockingly cold water. Her sodden tights were barely offering her any extra protection or warmth. As soon as Roger was out of sight, she sat on the embankment and lifted her now heavy legs from the water. The cold air seemed to bite at her toes and she was unsure which was better, to stand in the freezing water or hold her feet out of it.

Determined to concentrate on something else, she stared into the dusky night sky and watched the stars appear like little fireflies. It momentarily helped her take her mind off the pain in her legs. She frequently glanced across at the farmhouse, knowing Roger would turn on the porch light when he was on his way back. If he ever returned. This thought circled her ever-numbing brain and she began to wonder what she would do, where she could go if he didn't. She sighed heavily and watched her breath float out into the cold air, reassuring her that she was still alive. She moved her arms further into the sockets of her sweater, desperately trying to keep warm. Goosebumps covered her body. She wished she'd listened to her mother's constant nagging about wearing a thermal vest. Her legs and feet were so cold that they ached, so she tried to move around but they were becoming too numb and heavy to lift – she couldn't have run away if she'd wanted to. She gave up trying to move around and, getting her arms back into her sweater, she edged her way up the dyke. She managed to carefully and slowly put each numb foot either side of the small ditch. Eventually, she manoeuvred herself round to sitting, the smell of urine and murky stagnant water filling her nostrils. Pulling her arms back into her clothes, she grabbed whatever time she could to get warm.

Concentrating on the magical starry dome that encased the world, she began to wonder if there was anyone else enduring what she was at that very moment in time. Another young girl who looked like her, whose life was similar – she'd read a story about parallel worlds, she knew it was possible. Then she remembered her friend Arabella. Her dad was a bastard – they compared stories sometimes – but he did other things to her that thankfully Roger had never done to Cecelia. Yvonne was always telling Cecelia there was someone somewhere worse off than her or going through the same thing, and that she must be thankful for what she had and focus on the happy times.

She always said this with her tiny little Bible pressed hard between her fingers like a vice. It was all bollocks as far as Cecelia was concerned – she always wondered where her mother's god was when Roger was on top form. She'd found her asleep on the bathroom floor on more than one occasion, curled up, fully clothed and shivering where she'd been made to sleep all night. The Bible lay next to her and when Cecelia asked why she continued to read it as, given her circumstances, it clearly wasn't helping, she replied that we all have our cross to bear. Like Sebastian, Cecelia had begun to lose patience with Yvonne's pathetic attempts at assertiveness and it had begun to make her angrier and angrier.

A star so bright it reminded Cecelia of a Christmas light shone towards her. The little constellation twinkled, making her feel like she was the only one who could see it. She closed her eyes and made a wish.

'What are you doing?'

Cecelia, startled, quickly sunk her feet back into the water, as she looked up to see the outline of Roger's figure in the dusky bleakness. She was blinded by the torch he was shining in her face. She'd taken her eye off the porch door and he'd appeared, the sound of his movements hidden by the gusting wind. Her heart hammered in her chest, her mouth was numb with cold and her words were stuck in her mind where there seemed to be a strike, unable to reach her mouth. She daren't move as he shone the torch on the rest of her body and she knew she'd be in trouble for having her arms tucked in her clothes. 'Come on, out you get!' Roger barked.

Cecelia could barely move she was so cold. The relief and fear that he'd returned was swirling around in her stomach like an unappetising soup. She was beginning to root into the thick mud like a shrub.

Roger's long legs straddled the narrow ditch. He grabbed her and she stumbled forward onto her front, unable to put her hands out to save herself. The side of her face and her shoulder took the brunt of the fall and she bit her lip in the process. Salty tears tumbled down her face as she silently cried at the pain that was turning into a smouldering ache across her already sore heart.

Roger laughed, grabbed the back of her damp sweater and dragged her onto the field.

'Cold, are we?'

They walked back to the house, Cecelia desperately trying to keep up with his stride. She felt like a bound hostage with her arms tucked in her school shirt and sweater.

They neared one of the hangars that always made her shudder. To her surprise, on this occasion he dragged her straight into the house. The relief that rose inside her was so overwhelming she sobbed again and more tears leaked into the dirty graze on her face. Maybe, just maybe, she thought, he was going to leave her punishment at that. Then it dawned on her that Yvonne might be waiting inside for her and that was why he was bringing her in. Could it be that enduring a punishment had magically reversed the last week and brought Yvonne back to life? Her tears briefly subsided as she was steered into the kitchen and she searched the room, expectant and hopeful. But of course, Yvonne wasn't there. And, as quickly as she'd been shoved into the kitchen, she was briskly marched upstairs to the bathroom. He was going to warm her in the tub, she thought, but not in the gentle way her mother did.

'Strip down to your bra and pants.'

She did as she was told, albeit slowly, her muscles tight with fear and cold, teeth chattering noisily, horrors of Arabella's stories resounding in her ears. She watched the steaming water thunder into the old enamel bath, willing him to turn on the cold tap.

'Get in. Come on! You want to warm up, don't you? I'm not having those busy bodies saying I've neglected you.'

The water from the tap was hot but not scalding and under normal circumstances Yvonne would run her a bath solely on that. But, when you were almost perished, it felt like burning embers. Her tiny, damp, bluish coloured feet, flecked with bits of dirt from the ditch, were slowly placed into the water. She bit her bottom lip so hard with the pain that she made it bleed. The metallic sharpness felt comforting to her, a release in her mute world. She closed her eyes as she waited for the sharp, stabbing pains in her legs and feet to subside. If she got through this without too much fuss, Roger would leave her alone for the rest of the evening.

Eventually, her legs and feet began to warm painlessly and she longed to plunge the rest of her icy cold body into the water. But Roger was watching her, seeing the proceedings through to the bitter end. There was no heating in the bathroom and she could see her breath escaping through her chattering teeth now that the steam from the bath had subsided.

'Get out and dry yourself. It's time for you to get ready for bed.' He left the room and she heard his footsteps pound the corridor. His tone had sounded dark and she knew from experience that his initial elation at punishing her had worn off. He was bored and Cecelia was relieved.

Letting out a large breath of air she watched the steam drift through the atmosphere, knowing she was still alive. A tug in her stomach rose to her chest, pulling her heart into her throat as it dawned on her again that her mother wasn't there. Cecelia and Sebastian, alone in their small world.

A light tapping on the bathroom door made her look up and she held her breath again as she waited to see who was there. Sebastian tiptoed in, put his finger to his lips, a signal to her that he wouldn't speak since they both knew that if Roger caught them he would be in even more trouble than she was. Silently he walked towards her, a hot cup of Bovril steaming in his hands. A huge well of despair rose in Cecelia's chest and she began to sob. Sebastian placed the mug on the top of the toilet seat and pulled her into his arms.

'It's OK, Mouse.' He kissed the top of her damp hair. 'It's going to be all right.'

The feel of his hands always warmed her, reassured her, but it was a superficial safeness – she always had that edgy feeling it wasn't going to be all right. Nothing was ever going to be all right.

For quite some time after, Cecelia waited in bed for Roger to come and check on her, but he didn't. She dozed for a while, and when she heard the click of his bedroom door she knew she was safe. She quietly and carefully tiptoed across her room and opened the door to the small loft space. Even though she was tired and weary, it was something she had to do. Sitting on the purlin in the draughty little attic dispersed something within her. Just a few minutes, she told herself. She stepped neatly into the dark cavern, pausing every few seconds to listen for Roger. Satisfied that he had settled she pulled herself along the wooden beam. She bent her leg and lifted her pyjama trouser leg above her knee. She liked the feel of her mouth on her tight skin. It comforted her and reminded her of Yvonne, although she didn't know why.

Steadying her breath, she tried to get used to the dark, cold atmosphere that was absorbing her; flashbacks of her time in the ditch causing her heart to beat faster. This was the only place she didn't mind the blackness. She stared into the abyss, her peripheral view picking up shapes and light. Her eyes widened as she tried to see the end of the long narrow loft space, something she often did. Even the light from the open loft door didn't stretch to the end. As she looked away again her vision caught the outline of a shape, but when she looked straight on, she couldn't see anything. Turning her head away again she could definitely see a large rectangular shape resting on the beam. She edged along the purlin but knew from experience that going too far would mean she wouldn't hear if Roger came in. She stopped wriggling and stared into the empty darkness. There it was again as she twisted her head to look behind her. She paused and stared back into the darkness, wanting to go on and look but frightened of Roger stirring. Curiosity getting the better of her, she wiggled her bottom forward. Allowing her eyes to adjust to the deeper darkness, she suddenly had a better look at what the shape was. It was a green suitcase that she'd never noticed there before, but that seemed sort of familiar to her. It was out of reach so, cold and tired, she decided to go back to her bedroom and explore the loft the following night when she would be armed with a torch.

The sudden sound of a door closing in the distance made her heart pound even more than it already had been. She edged backwards like a cornered animal. In her haste, she almost lost her balance as she turned and a small whimper escaped her lips. The only sound she'd uttered in two weeks.

Without waiting to hear if Roger was coming, she scrambled through the door, shut it firmly behind her and jumped into bed, pulling the covers up over her head. She lay there desperately trying to calm her rapid breathing and panicked heart. It was only when she had calmed did she notice how sore her chapped legs and feet were.

After a short while she pulled the duvet from her head and as she did so she heard the unmistakable click of her father's bedroom door. She wondered if he'd come into her room unheard.

Cecelia lay there staring into the darkness as it moved across the room, smothering her with its cold, viscous breath. Her heartbeat responded as panic began to rise in her chest and spilled from her eyes, as she thought about her mother once more.

Yvonne's face floated in the inky blackness and Cecelia reached out her hand to grasp it, knowing all too well it was a figment of her imagination.

She turned over in the bed and concentrated on the blotchy Anaglypta wallpaper, picking out imaginary shapes of elves and fairies as Yvonne had taught her to do when she was a small child and afraid of the dark. A few moments later the green suitcase swirled around in her subconscious as she slept fitfully, wondering why it was there. She dreamt she was balancing on the purlin like a gymnast on a beam. As she pirouetted she turned to see Yvonne floating in the loft space, her face pale and panic stricken. Then the purlin snapped, sending Cecelia and the case plummeting through the murky depths of blackness. She woke with a start, heart thundering in her chest, to find Roger standing over her, his face lit up by the moon shining through the window, mouth set in a straight line and his blue eyes dark and emotionless.

'What's up, Mouse?'

6

As much as it pained him to know Cecelia was outside suffering, Sebastian knew he needed to use the time Roger was with her outside to search the house. He was looking for their mother, even though the dragging sensation in his chest was telling him she wasn't there. Her pale bare feet with mucky soles appeared in his head, the memory of her lying under the kitchen table never present when he tried to recall it, but easily flashing in front of him at unexpected moments, like someone springing from a dark alley.

Frantically he ran from room to room, looking under the beds, in the wardrobes, behind doors – ridiculous places, he knew that. Searching for Yvonne, their mother, the person who already seemed pale and faded.

Sebastian had always seen something different in Yvonne – a prettiness in her eyes that told him there had been a time when her hair was shiny, her skin bright and glowing. Over the last couple of years Sebastian's relationship with his mother had struggled to stay the same. It had all changed when Sebastian had begun to spend more time on the farm as Roger demanded his help during the busy seasons, forcing him to prioritise the farm over his schoolwork, just as Roger had when he was a boy. Sebastian had become disheartened as he saw more of his mother's vulnerabilities. She had a weakness about her that he'd once wanted to protect, but recently he had found himself irritated by this lack of strength – seeing her as pathetic. This was only highlighted by the fact that as Cecelia got older she fought back more. Yvonne's inability to stand up to Roger had made Sebastian dislike her, but he loved her all the same.

Upon reflection, they'd all changed. Cecelia's involuntary muteness was more and more frequent, closing her off from the world, and even from him in lots of ways. Sebastian and Yvonne were the only people Cecelia could communicate with – Sebastian, in particular, could read everything on her face. A few years ago they'd found a book on sign language in the library and taught themselves the basics. This allowed him a way into her mind – his favourite place, their private world that no one else understood. He could see it all now as he watched Roger from the hall window marching across the yard, back to the house.

Pausing in his frenzied search, Sebastian knew he wouldn't find his mother. Roger had removed all trace of her, was pretending she'd packed up all her stuff and had left. But Sebastian knew this wasn't true.

Ten minutes later Sebastian found himself walking through the town towards the police station. He mechanically opened the heavy weighted door and stood in the reception area waiting for the desk sergeant to finish his telephone call. All he could think about was the strong smell of dusty old office files, disinfectant and cigarettes. Focus on what you're here for, he told himself, but all of a sudden his mind was blank and he couldn't think why he was there. Yvonne, you're here for your mother; he pushed his feet together, making sure the toes of his trainers were exactly in line.

'You all right there, lad?' Sebastian looked up to see the police officer leaning over the desk to see what he was staring at so intently. He stepped forward carefully.

'What can we do for you?'

'I think my father has killed someone . . .'

There was a flicker of a smile before the sergeant answered and Sebastian wondered if he could land him a decent punch through the narrow gap of the sliding glass panels.

'What makes you think that?'

'Can I see someone about it?' Sebastian felt himself rise in his trainers.

'As soon as you give me a few more details. Who is your father supposed to have killed?'

Sebastian turned and fought with the doors to escape, wanting to kick himself for pulling the handle instead of pushing it as the sign clearly said. His confidence dispersed along with each breath in the cold early evening air.

'Just a minute, lad, what's your name?' he heard the police officer call after him.

Lad, boy, the names that were always used by adults when they referred to him – showing their authority, placing him beneath them. Roger did it, so did his teachers. The teachers probably couldn't even remember his name. And just for the twenty minutes it took him to walk back to the farm, he felt that he didn't know who he was either, or where he belonged.

Where have you been, greeted him upon his return. Fuck off Roger, was his response as he made his way into the kitchen to make Cecelia a hot drink. And for the first time in his life, his father left him alone, allowing him to walk away, but noting his behaviour for another day.

7

As the twins approached their fifteenth birthday, school had become a safe haven for Cecelia and her temper. Unlike the other students there, she didn't ever want the school day to end. Everything was contained, structured, in bite-size pieces that she could cope with. She became the last one out of the gates, when previously she'd been the first. She'd always been desperate to see her mother at the end of the day, but now there was no one to go home to apart from Sebastian and she saw him at school. Even the sanctuary of her tiny room had been taken away. After seeing the green suitcase, she'd come home from school the next day to find her bedroom completely rearranged. Where the small door to the tiny loft had been was now a smooth wall and her chest of drawers had been moved in front of it. Roger had tried to pretend he'd given her room a much needed clean. New start, he had said. Best you adjust to the change and stop being reminded of things you can't have, he'd winked at her. Her posters had been taken down and ripped in half, neatly placed on top of her desk, infuriating her even more. Rifling through her school bag, she'd located a lighter, ignited the ruined posters and thrown them out of her bedroom window to ease her rage.

And now, all these months hidden away, the unopened letter continued to stare at her defiantly where it had been leant up against her bedside lamp again. She hovered near it, the lighter still aflame, but she knew if she destroyed it, regret would tug at her afterwards. Instead, she shut her drawer and ignored the pull of the envelope.

During the last few months a routine had developed: Cecelia would lose her temper and lash out and would then be punished, or Sebastian would forget to do something on the farm and would be similarly abused. Cecelia was pushing Roger, seeing how far he would go, how much he would hurt her. She didn't know why but she immensely enjoyed the anger it fired in him.

When not doing this, Cecelia and Sebastian spent most of their time together. They'd become even closer since Yvonne had gone, clinging to each other for comfort. Most evenings, once Roger had fallen asleep in front of the television, Cecelia would run herself a bath or join Sebastian if he was already in there. They'd always bathed together, sharing the water, something Roger had tried to stop as they grew older. One at a time, he always chastised – it's not right at your age. They ignored him. It was space they used to catch up, make plans and reassure each other. If they weren't both in the bath, one would be bathing while the other sat on an old wooden chair, chirping away like birds, the warmth from the water lifting their spirits. Part of the excitement was the risk that Roger would catch them, but he never stirred once he'd fallen asleep.

The comfort of the bathroom had replaced that of the kitchen – it was a safe place in the house free from their father. Roger didn't approve of nudity and, giggling like children, Cecelia and Sebastian would often dare one another to wander through the house naked, just to wind him up. Neither of them had ever been shy – they'd been exhibitionists when they were children and neither of their parents could understand who they had inherited this trait from. At any given opportunity they would both strip off and wander around freely, giggling at one another.

The bathroom was also the only place where Cecelia spoke. Her voice had returned a few days previously on her way home from school when she'd shouted at a boy throwing conkers at people. It had been the longest she'd been mute and she'd become so used to not speaking that she was still refusing to talk to anyone apart from Sebastian, enjoying the safety of her secret silence.

Cecelia got up from the chair she'd been sitting on while she dried her toes and listened to Sebastian talk about his day. She allowed the towel to drop onto the floor as she pulled on her bathrobe. She kicked it across the floor and yanked the other towels off the drying rack to join the others in the pile.

'Everything stinks in this house. I'm going downstairs to do some washing.'

'Leave me a towel.' He leant forward and pulled out the plug. He would lie in the bath until the water emptied – something Cecelia couldn't understand. He said it made him feel solid again, brought his being to the forefront of his mind. She had tried it once, just to please him, but it had made her feel sluggish and heavy as she lay in the bottom of the empty tub. All she'd wanted to do was refill it with hot water, as she'd shivered against the cold enamel. Sebastian had wanted her to feel the transition of the gravity in her body. But all she'd been able to focus on was her pulse, which thumped through her stomach as her body sank lower into the tub.

'What's going on in here then?' Roger was blocking Cecelia's way as she opened the bathroom door.

Ignoring him, she pushed her way past and went downstairs to the utility room to load the dirty towels in the twin tub. Roger let her go, as he had often done lately since she'd started squaring up to him. The balance between them was shifting; her father was becoming aware of what she was capable of.

8

Sebastian didn't move from the bath. He was hoping that Roger would be too embarrassed by the sight of his naked body and would walk away without argument. He was surprised he hadn't followed Cecelia.

'It's disgusting,' he heard his father hiss. 'What you're doing is pure filth.'

'She's my sister, don't be so perverse.' Sebastian lifted his tall frame from the now empty bathtub. Cecelia had taken all the towels but he still searched the room in case there was one anywhere.

'Excuse me, I need to get a towel.' Sebastian tried to push past his father but Roger wouldn't budge.

'I want to talk to you.'

'I don't need a lecture; we're not doing anything wrong. We've always done this. You're seeing something that isn't there.' He tried again to push past Roger but he stood defiantly.

'Isn't there?' his voice was beginning to rise and Sebastian knew it would end in an argument. 'Do you know what people would say if they knew what you were doing!'

'I don't care what other people think. Do you know what people are saying about you? That our mother never left this farm; that you killed her. I'd be more worried about that if I were you.'

Sebastian had no idea where that had come from. It was as though someone had taken over his brain and was speaking for him. Now he was in trouble.

Roger grabbed Sebastian by his neck, bashing his head against the door frame. 'What did you just say to me, boy?' He was snarling in Sebastian's face like a rabid dog. Sebastian's vision was blurred from the blow to his head. Consciousness regained, he grabbed his father's arm with one hand and punched him in the face with the other. Within seconds they were fighting on the floor, more seriously than the grapples they had in the yard when Roger was trying to toughen him up.

Sebastian was naked and vulnerable and as their wrestling reached the top of the stairs, he took a kick between his legs, rendering him helpless for some moments. Roger regained his balance, grabbed Sebastian by his dark blond hair and dragged him down the first set of stairs. Once he reached the right-angled turn in the steps, his temper got the better of him and he continued to kick Sebastian. As Sebastian fell down the last set of stairs, he managed to reach out and grab Roger by the leg so he tumbled down with him. There was a bang and a crack as Roger hit his head on one of the spindles in the banister, snapping it in two.

At the bottom of the stairs, Sebastian and Roger slumped like logs split with an axe. Eventually, Roger stood up, unsteady on his feet as he touched the gash on his forehead and looked at the blood on his fingertips. Sebastian pulled himself across the floor so he could lean against the wall in an attempt to stop the room from spinning.

You're nothing but scum, were the last words he heard from Roger's lips. There was a flicker of movement in the dark shadow of the large hallway and Sebastian looked up to see Cecelia standing there, her bathrobe open, revealing her naked form. It was a few seconds before he noticed she was holding the .22 rifle from the gun cabinet. And many moments later before he was aware of Roger's body slumped on the stairs and the blood that had sprayed gently up the wall behind him.

Sebastian slowly turned to look at Cecelia as she tipped the rifle up, unscrewed the silencer, and walked back into the kitchen.

It shocked him that he found the image so erotic and yet, he couldn't explain why.

9

Cecelia made her way to school the next day as normal, although she didn't get very far. They had to be normal, Sebastian had said. There was a relief in her body she couldn't help wallow in; it was clear in her face and the way she moved. She couldn't think about the horror of what she'd done the previous night. That way she could feel safe in her mute world. Sebastian had said they would decide later what they'd do next. Roger had abused them all and then Cecelia had shot him – a fair deal as far as she was concerned.

'We must carry on as we have been since Mum disappeared. OK?' Sebastian pulled at her sweater, making her stop in the street. She nodded, reassuring him by squeezing his arm.

'I need time to think about what we're going to do. How we're going to deal with the situation.'

Cecelia thought of Roger still lying at the bottom of the stairs, the top half of his body positioned awkwardly. She remembered thinking how uncomfortable it must be as she'd stared at him while eating her toast. Taking a tissue from her school bag, she'd covered his face with it, not wanting to look at his wide-open, empty eyes. They'd decided not to move him for now. Sebastian had told her not to touch him or use that staircase; they would have to use the one situated across the other side of the house.

Cecelia had lit the fire and they'd slept on the couches in the sitting room. Strangely, it had been the most restful night's sleep she'd had for months. Her mind was calm, settled, even though in the distance, the far scenery of her mind, she knew what she'd done wasn't quite right. She'd killed someone and it didn't matter why. It was still wrong, but she couldn't quite grasp how wrong it was. There was something in her that simply didn't care. Not even when she'd woken the following day and stepped over Roger's legs to get to the kitchen.

Sebastian grabbed her arm, stopping her in her tracks again. 'Maybe we shouldn't go to school ... perhaps we ought to go back ... hide in the house or barns until someone comes?'

She could see he was running through the ideas, trying to find the right one as they spilled from his mouth.

Cecelia shrugged.

'They'll know how long he's been dead. When it's investigated ...'

'Let's get rid of him. The grain store or something?'

Sebastian frowned at her. 'Where he could be easily found? For fuck's sake Cece, is that the best you can come up with?'

'OK. What's your marvellous plan then?'

He stepped closer to her. She wasn't going to like what he was about to say.

'We can't get rid of him, Mouse ... we can't get rid of him because ... look, I've had an idea. We could make it look like Mum did it ...'

Cecelia was shaking her head before he'd even finished the sentence and began walking back to school. 'No way,' she snapped at him.

Sebastian fell into step beside her so she turned round and began walking towards the farm, tears pouring down her face.

'Mouse, Cece, listen to me. It's our way out of this mess. If the police think either one of us shot Roger,' he lowered his voice, even though there was nobody around to hear, 'we will be separated and one of us will be going to a young offenders prison. Mum would want this for us, don't you see? We'll say she came back and a few days later we heard an argument between her and Roger . . .'

Cecelia glared at him, walking faster. He'd stepped too far across the line for her. She would not have their mother taking the blame for something she hadn't done. Even if she was dead, Cecelia didn't want to have her remembered as a murderer, especially after what had happened that day.

Sebastian grabbed hold of Cecelia's school bag, stopping her from walking. She wrenched herself free from his grip.

'This is the only way, Cecelia. Mum would want this, I know it.'

'How do you know what Mum would have wanted? You have no idea, no idea whatsoever about anything that went on in that house.' Cecelia almost spat in his face, she was so angry. 'That's what she'll be remembered for and I'm not having it, I'd rather turn myself in.'

'She's dead, Cece!' Sebastian grabbed her school bag, wrenching her back towards him. 'Mum is dead and this is the only way. Don't let him ruin the rest of our lives as well.'

Cecelia didn't like what he was saying, but she knew he was right. She continued back to the farm where Sebastian helped her bury the gun and silencer deep in one of the ditches that Roger had made her stand in.

A short while later, realising they had to tell someone their version of what had happened, they called the police. Sebastian prayed the officer he'd seen in the station wasn't on shift. They sat on the sofa holding each other and waited for someone to come. Differing stories of past events swirling around in their minds, they were both hiding secrets but only one of them thought they knew the truth.

10

A week later, Cecelia was holding Sebastian's hand tightly as they sat in the back of the social worker's car and pulled up outside an all too familiar house. They both knew this part of town; it was an area they passed every day on the way to and from school, occasionally taking a detour up a narrow, steep alleyway which led to the local graveyard, putting off the inevitable return to White Horse Farm.

They'd never known when they were younger that the children they played with from the house had been foster kids. They hadn't been bothered to ask and were more interested in the newsagent's and fish and chip shop further up the high street. The house belonged to a woman called Eleanor who lived there with her son, Samuel. It had been in the family for years – her brother had run a funeral directors there but he had died recently. Samuel, who was in his mid-twenties, was trying to take over the business.

Cecelia knew Yvonne didn't like Eleanor and Samuel and hadn't approved of her and Sebastian going to the house – making the excuse that the place attracted unsavoury characters – but Cecelia liked it there. She felt at home and had always got on well with

Eleanor, even though she'd met some odd children there. Eleanor was an easy person to talk to – softly spoken, attentive, a wise beacon in Cecelia's confused world.

Looking at the house now, Cecelia thought about all the foster children who'd stayed there and wondered if any of their situations had been similar to theirs. Now they had become the mystery behind the windows, instead of the onlookers outside.

Cecelia recalled Ava and Imogen, twins who had lived in the house and who she and Sebastian had befriended during primary school. They'd drifted towards them when they'd first arrived at the school – twins subconsciously drawn to each other and into their strange secret world that other children didn't understand. Cecelia had been envious that the girls had a bedroom in the loft space and she would often ponder what could have been if Sebastian had been a female twin instead of male. Would they have been allowed to share a room? Were same sex twins even closer? Then she decided that Imogen was too competitive with Ava and the envy had quickly dispersed.

Ava and Imogen were mirror twins. They often spoke at the same time and even wore the same clothes. Sebastian had found them weird, creepy he said, and decided not to spend time at the house anymore, but Cecelia had been intrigued by them. They were more than identical, but she didn't understand what mirror twins meant. Ever since then she'd thought she and Sebastian were mirror twins. She knew they couldn't be, biologically, but in personality they reflected one another. She liked being around Ava and Imogen; even though she was the extra limb outside their secret world, it intrigued her to see what others saw when they looked at her and Sebastian. She'd also never experienced being singular before.

Then, one day when they'd been playing a game in the garden, Cecelia discovered why Sebastian had thought the twins were so peculiar. Ava and Imogen were always swapping and pretending to be one another – they thought it was funny because no one could really tell them apart. Cecelia could, though, because she always thought Imogen had a slightly different look in her eye to Ava. It was the shape of her irises, she realised later – they weren't as round, which Cecelia felt gave her a colder appearance.

They'd been playing a kind of hide and seek game that Cecelia hadn't heard of before where once you'd been discovered you were chased by the finder. Cecelia remembered it being a very long garden, quite narrow, and at the bottom it spread out into a small orchard with the graveyard beyond. She'd loved the way the trees seemed to be in uniform order, offering a tent-like shade in the summer. Right at the very bottom was an old war bunker, partly dug into the ground; Cecelia had been fascinated at being able to run her hands over the grass-covered roof. Inside felt very different – it was sharply cold with a heavy darkness; small compartments ran off the tunnel.

It was Cecelia's turn to search and as soon as she braved her way down there, having exhausted all other options, she'd immediately wanted to come straight out, the darkness being too much of a reminder of home, a more claustrophobic version of the hangars on the farm. But she'd heard giggling in the blackness and a strange scraping noise. Her eagerness to win had gotten the better of her. Found you, she called, in the hope that one or both would come out, so she didn't have to venture any further inside, even though she knew neither girl would allow her to flout the rules.

Cecelia saw the faint glow of light before she heard them both call in unison, 'we're in here!' Arms outstretched, not wanting to be called a scaredy cat, she made her way further into the tunnel. The glow of light faded and died and she couldn't see anything. All she could think about was what would happen if the bunker caved in on them. More scraping echoed off the white walls followed by a glow and she realised the girls were lighting matches. Panic filled her as the light faded again and she screamed as she was grabbed and pulled into one of the small caverns.

'We're playing a game,' Imogen said, although Cecelia couldn't be sure it was her in the dim light.

Disoriented, Cecelia was pulled back by her neck as one of the girls put what she thought was a cotton bag over her head, and held it tight around the base, making it difficult for Cecelia to breathe. Her hands grasped at the cloth as she desperately tried to draw breath, but they just wrenched her closer to the floor, so she was incapable of doing anything. All she could hear was the two of them giggling.

'Cece doesn't like the scarf game,' one girl said to the other and they began to laugh again.

Just as Cecelia thought she was going to pass out, they pulled the scarf from her head and dropped her onto the floor. Crawling from the bunker as she tried to get her breath back, she ran all the way home and never went back again. A few weeks later Ava and Imogen disappeared from the school, and she later learned they'd left Eleanor's house as well.

'Do you remember those weird girls who lived here?' Sebastian said, looking up at the top floor window as the social worker parked the car.

Cecelia squeezed his hand.

'I fancied one of them . . . Imogen I think it was.'

'You told me you thought they were weird.'

'They were. I once found them in that old war bunker, naked . . .' Sebastian lowered his voice so the social worker wouldn't hear.

'Oh. That's why you fancied one of them, is it?' Cecelia was trying to be light-hearted but there was an edge to her voice that surprised even her.

Sebastian gave her a sidelong glance, smiling at her, knowing there was a hint of jealousy. They both looked up to see the social worker looking at them curiously in the mirror.

'Are you two going to get out?'

'You're supposed to come in with us, aren't you?' Cecelia released Sebastian's hand.

'Afraid not, I have another appointment. You'll be OK; your visit went well the other day. They're expecting you.'

Standing on the path, Sebastian lifted the large ornate knocker, letting it hit the door with one resounding bang. Cecelia felt so tiny, standing in front of the imposing Victorian house.

'What were they doing in the war bunker naked?' Cecelia whispered.

Sebastian looked directly at her. 'What do you think they were doing, Cece?'

11

The loft room was almost like an apartment; Cecelia had been sharing it with another foster girl, a surly creature she didn't really get on with. When she'd left, Sebastian hadn't been allowed to move in with Cecelia – Samuel had said it wasn't a good idea. Sebastian laughed about it with Cecelia. They thought it was ridiculous since his bedroom was just a few short steps below the loft room and they were still permitted to share a bathroom.

'Did you notice Eleanor didn't say we couldn't share? It's because Samuel fancies you,' Sebastian had teased Cecelia. He'd joked about this when they'd first arrived and Samuel had been very attentive to her needs. Now it wasn't so funny.

'There's someone else arriving in a couple of days – a girl called Leyla . . . Lola, something like that anyway.' Cecelia had chosen to ignore his comment.

Sebastian had noticed she'd been spending more and more time with Samuel – helping him with the business – and in turn he'd been overseeing some of her coursework. Sebastian would tease her just to see her reaction; he was jealous and struggling to hide it. Cecelia reassured him he was being ridiculous but it hadn't been the response he was looking for.

It was important to Sebastian that the time he spent with Cecelia was concentrated, filled with interesting conversation and laughter, maintaining their closeness. He didn't want her to forget what they shared and drift towards someone else. Having only one bathroom between them had been a rare stroke of luck because the bathroom was where they had always shared some of their best moments.

Sebastian had taken to drawing Cecelia while he sat in the bath and she on an old wooden chair while she talked to him. It had come about when he'd been doing some art homework in the tub one day, resting his sketch book on the bath rack and, distracted by his sister, he'd begun to draw her and it was something he'd enjoyed doing ever since.

The house was much larger than Sebastian remembered; a grand entrance hall with a stripped wooden floor, partly covered by an Indian rug, led up to a curved and austere staircase. Sebastian felt that the people didn't fit in the house and the house didn't seem to like its inhabitants. When they'd first arrived it was warmly lit and welcoming, but now they'd settled in it felt superficial and slightly cold.

'How can she afford a house like this?' Sebastian whispered to Cecelia one night when they were in the sitting room.

'She and her brother inherited it, but now he's gone it's been left to her. That's what Samuel told me. Anyway, why wouldn't she have a house like this?'

'I don't know. It just doesn't suit them, I suppose . . .'

For the first time in their lives Cecelia and Sebastian's opinions about other people differed. He could see she felt comfort from the family routine they offered. He didn't though. Cecelia was his family and she was all he needed.

'What are we going to do when we've finished here, Cece?' Sebastian asked her as he sat in the bath later that evening, sketching his sister's face as she concentrated hard on painting her nails. Cecelia frowned, changing the balance of her face, the perplexed expression causing her mouth to tip to one side.

'I don't think we need to look beyond tomorrow. Let's see what comes our way and stay in the moment.'

Sebastian stopped what he was doing. 'Could you try and think for yourself at some point.' He flicked water at her.

'I do!'

'You sound like a robotic version of Eleanor . . . turn your face towards me slightly. Stop frowning.'

'And you,' Cecelia stood up from her chair, her towel falling slightly, revealing her back and side, the ridges of her ribs, reminding him of the church etchings they used to do at primary school, 'sound like Leonardo bloody de Vinci. I don't know what we're going to do, Sebastian. What do you think we should do?'

Watching Cecelia getting dressed, Sebastian observed her shape, so different from his own. The sharing of skin and cells always comforted him, made him feel close to her.

'Once we turn sixteen, we can find somewhere to live on our own.'

'What with? We don't have any money.'

'I'm going to take on a market stall, expand on the stuff I've been selling at school.'

Cecelia sat back down in her chair. 'Socks?! What about your studies? You can't do that as well, you won't have time.'

'Yes, I will. I'm going to college to study art, I've decided not to take my A levels.'

'That's ridiculous! While we have a roof over our heads we may as well make use of it until we're asked to leave; study hard and get some qualifications behind us. Selling thermal underwear isn't going to pay our bills.'

'You're forgetting something. Once we turn sixteen, we won't be welcome in this house anymore.'

'Yes we will; they won't throw us out . . .' Cecelia shook the small bottle of varnish and started on her toes. 'And anyway, there's always the farm . . .'

'No,' Sebastian said firmly, turning back to his sketchbook now that Cecelia was sitting down again. He could see a question hovering on her lips, the words, like spiders, crept from her mouth but she said nothing. There would never be a time when he wanted to return to his childhood home – it filled him with a heavy darkness he didn't want to think about.

'I'm going into town later; I need to buy some linen.'

'Uh huh, what for?' Cecelia pressed her lips to her bare knee and he wondered why she always did that.

'A new technique I want to try out for my coursework.'

'Oh. Will I be needed as a guinea pig?'

Movement on the stairs made Sebastian look up. Cecelia followed his gaze and turned in her chair. Both of them stared at the closed bathroom door. Sebastian put his finger to his lips and Cecelia tiptoed quietly into the separate shower cubicle situated in the corner of the room.

Sebastian pulled himself from the bath water, wrapped a towel around his waist and opened the door. Samuel stood there, hands in his jean pockets.

'Why didn't you knock?'

'Is Cecelia in there with you?'

'No. What do you want?'

'I just want to speak to her about something.'

'Sorry, I don't know where she is.' Sebastian closed the door to find it immediately pushed open again.

'Do you need some money?'

'Sorry?'

'Take some money.' Samuel pushed a five pound note into Sebastian's hand.

'What's this for?'

'You might need it . . .'

Sebastian stood there, baffled. He'd been expecting a lecture about him and Cecelia spending too much time in the bathroom.

'Breakfast is on the table. Can you let Cece know, please?'

Sebastian watched him make his way down the corridor. He could feel the draught lift slightly at Samuel's reference to Cecelia's shortened name. The name only Sebastian used for her.

'That was nice of him.' Cecelia crept out of the shower cubicle.

Sebastian frowned. 'No it wasn't; he's fucking weird.'

'No he's not. They're just making sure we have everything we need . . . they didn't have to take us in, Sebastian.'

'Oh, fuck off, Cece! Eleanor's a foster parent, out for what she can get – don't think they're not being paid to have us here. They don't give a toss about us.'

'Yes they do, you're being really unkind. It makes a change to be part of a normal family.'

'Ha!' Sebastian laughed, wandering into his bedroom to get dressed. It was pointless returning to his bath, the moment was lost. 'You better hurry up and get down there for breakfast before it gets cold.'

Upon returning to his room, he found a local newspaper lying on his bed. It was folded in half, the headline read, 'Woman's body found in woodland near White Horse Farm'.

12

When Cecelia returned to the loft room she found a small bag of chocolates on her bed with a note which read, *to help you with your studies*, the initial S underneath. She picked it up and stared at it, an unfamiliar feeling forming in her stomach. Samuel had been helping her with some coursework she'd been stuck on. He'd attended a private school when he was younger, where they had a different way of teaching; Cecelia found it more interesting, an easier way to learn facts.

'Have you read this?' Sebastian barged in waving a newspaper at her.

'Read what? I can't see if you don't hold it still.' She reached up and snatched it from him. She read it and then read it again. The room seemed to tilt one way, then the other.

'What's that?' Sebastian pointed to the chocolate and note on the bed, his voice slightly high-pitched.

Cecelia didn't answer. Sebastian snatched the note from her bedspread as she scanned the article.

'This is fucking weird.'

'You're telling me,' Cecelia whispered, the green suitcase on the purlin floating around in her mind.

'You don't even eat chocolate.'

Cecelia looked up, realising they were talking about different things.

'I think we've got far more important things to worry about than some stupid chocolates . . . where did you get this from?'

'What?' Sebastian frowned, exasperated by her attitude.

'The newspaper.'

'Is that all you're bothered about? Where the bloody newspaper came from. Aren't you more worried that the body could be Mum? Did you already know about this?'

'Eleanor told me yesterday.'

Sebastian held his hands out questioningly. She could see he was annoyed and getting ready to lecture her again, as he frequently had since they'd arrived at the house. He kept saying he felt like he was losing her, but he couldn't see that his constant bombardment was pushing her away.

'I didn't tell you because it might not have anything to do with us. In fact . . . I know it's not Mother so don't worry about it.'

'How do you know?'

'I just do, all right. Trust me. Someone told me it's a drug addict from the brothel down by the station.'

'Who told you that?'

'Never mind who told me, you can be rest assured it's not Mother, it's just some old whore someone just happened to dump on the farm. Now don't keep questioning me.'

'Oh, I knew this would happen.'

'What?' Cecelia got up from her bed and began putting her clean washing away.

Sebastian reached forward and tugged at her arm. 'Don't do this, Cece. Don't close yourself off from me . . .'

'You're being silly, Sebastian, you're just tired.' Cecelia turned to look at him; she reached forward and touched his face. 'This is a big adjustment; it's not easy for either of us.'

'Do you ever think about Dad?'

Cecelia snatched her hands from his face and continued to hang up her clothes.

'You can't pretend –'

'No, I don't think about him or what happened . . . sorry, but I don't.' She shrugged defensively. Of course, there were times when she was going to sleep, unable to fill her head with anything else, when she did think about it, but in the main she didn't. Perhaps there was something amiss; in the outer recesses of her mind she knew she was somehow devoid of emotion, but she couldn't engage with any of it. It was the abuse, the humiliation, the mental manipulation that had made her cold towards her father and resulted in her shooting him. That's what she kept telling herself, but somewhere inside she knew the justification was a signal there was something very wrong. Or maybe the need to justify it told her she was normal; she'd long since given up thinking about it.

'I'm struggling with it . . . I need you.'

'Struggling with what?' Cecelia sat on the bed next to Sebastian and embraced him, unable to hide the exasperation in her voice.

'We killed our father . . .' Sebastian said quietly, looking round to make sure they were alone.

Cecelia sighed. '*We* didn't do anything. If you remember, it had nothing to do with you. So, there you go, you can forget about it and let me live with what happened. Because I can live with it. I really am all right, so just forget it. We've moved on and I don't want to hear the subject mentioned ever again.'

'Mention what?' Lola came running in and threw herself on her bed under the window. 'Come on, tell me. It all sounds very serious. What have you done?'

'Nothing.' Sebastian pulled himself from Cecelia and went downstairs to his own room, slamming the door behind him.

'What's got into him?'

'He's talking about giving up his studies so we can get a place of our own. That's all.'

'Does he have a girlfriend?'

'What's that got to do with anything?' Cecelia, having finished hanging her clothes up, turned her gaze on Lola.

'I just wondered, that's all.'

Cecelia realised Lola was looking for someone to chat to. Cecelia had seen other girls doing this at school, but had rarely taken part due to her temperamental voice – which strangely hadn't deserted her since her father had died. Being the observer for many years, she found small talk irritating and pointless.

'Sebastian doesn't need a girlfriend, he's got me,' she snapped, slamming the wardrobe door.

'Weird . . .' Lola whispered, rolling her eyes and turning her attention to the magazine on her bedside table.

Within moments Cecelia found herself across Lola's bed, her hand around the girl's thin neck as she rammed her up against the wall.

'I'm sorry, I'm sorry, I didn't mean it!'

'You better fucking not have.' Cecelia released her grip.

Lola's brown eyes were huge, filled with shock and fear. Cecelia grabbed the small girl, wrapped her arms around her slight frame and covered her head in kisses.

'I'm so sorry, I am really, really sorry,' she said over and over again, tightening her grip, harder and harder, dispersing her temper until she thought she might crush the girl to death.

13

Sebastian spread the roll of linen across the kitchen table and began cutting it into large sections, the headline from the newspaper flashing across his vision, dancing through his mind, worrying him. Eleanor had chosen to tell Cecelia about the body that was found and Cecelia had only thought to tell him when he'd asked who had left the newspaper in his room. It was bothering him. He wondered if his hostility towards Eleanor and Samuel made him too unapproachable – that's what Cecelia kept telling him anyway. They were too nice in his opinion and something was amiss – he'd never met anyone like them before. But whenever he tried to discuss it with his sister she just said they were good people, and he just wasn't used to it. And yet, everything about them irritated him: Samuel's band, the gigs he went to in the evenings, the funeral business, his clothes, the way he spoke. It made Sebastian want to punch him in the face. Eleanor was just as nice but less patronising, her voice more monotone, although, like Samuel, it was as though she was programmed to speak in a certain way. There was something about Eleanor that held his interest though. She had the most symmetrical face he'd ever seen. She wasn't the most attractive woman – her nose was too thin and it made her eyes appear too close together – but she held a calm confidence that was visible in her strong features, her long blond hair, like she had the answers to the wonders of the universe. Nothing seemed to faze her; she just floated through the house with the same aura each day. When Sebastian had stormed into the sitting room, aggressively throwing the newspaper across the floor, Eleanor hadn't flinched or changed her tone of voice or her attitude towards him. This was why she had such a good reputation as a foster parent. Cecelia was right – he wasn't used to people like that.

They were now both in the kitchen, Eleanor behind him, quietly minding her own business, chopping herbs on the worktop.

'Drink this.' She placed a mug on the table near to him.

'What is it?' He peered into the steaming cup of water, green leaves floating on the top.

'It's a calmer; it'll help you to focus on what you're doing.'

'Thanks.' Sebastian cautiously picked up the cup, sniffing the contents. 'Is it mint?'

'Yes, and a little lemon thyme.'

'What do all your rings mean? Do they have any significance?' Sebastian pointed to the large crystals covering almost every one of Eleanor's fingers. He was making an effort – trying to be nice to make a point to Cecelia.

'They all have some sort of health benefit. I usually wear the ones I'm drawn to and then change when the time feels right.'

'How do you know that the time is right?'

'Well, I usually feel slightly different, altered. Out of kilter I suppose you'd say. What's the linen for?'

'An art project . . . This is nice.' He lifted the cup towards her.

'I grow all the herbs in the orangery; just help yourself whenever you want some.' Eleanor moved forward and touched the linen.

'I'm trying to print parts of the body onto it using charcoals . . . possibly powder paints, I'm not sure yet.'

'Interesting. Need someone to try it out on?'

Sebastian hesitated. He was thinking about Cecelia; he'd really wanted to try it out on her first, as he always did with everything.

'I need to work out what I'm doing first. But thanks.' Sebastian began clearing up the pieces of material he'd already cut, and folded them around the roll of linen. That was enough for him for one day; he wasn't going to spend his entire Saturday with people he didn't particularly like. At the farm, they were all used to one another, it was easy to escape, snatch some time to yourself, but it was very different in this house. It always seemed like there was nowhere to go.

Eleanor sat down at the table and began dealing out some tarot cards, something she seemed to do on a daily basis, like it was a ritual.

'What do you get from looking at these?'

'Quite a lot, as it happens. I can see what's going on in the house, get a feel of the atmosphere.'

Sebastian nodded, unsure what she could possibly detect from a load of old cards. He remembered his mother visiting tarot readers or going to clairvoyant evenings at the town hall. She always came home slightly euphoric, hysterical almost. The fortunes that were told to her were always backed up by information the messenger couldn't have known. The joy this brought was always quickly destroyed by Roger, who ridiculed the whole event, and eventually his mother would plummet quite spectacularly and a dark mood would descend for days afterwards.

Sebastian recalled the last time Yvonne had visited a psychic. With all that had happened the last few months, he'd completely forgotten about it. Yvonne had arrived home and he and Cecelia were eagerly awaiting an update in the sitting room. They had loved the intrigue it stirred before Roger ruined it all. When Yvonne had got home she'd not said a word to anyone and had taken herself straight to bed. Cecelia and Sebastian wondered for quite some time about what she'd been told, but on this occasion, she had kept it to herself.

It was ironic that Cecelia and Sebastian had been placed in the care of a woman who appeared to have the same interests as their mother and in a house that Yvonne had never approved of them visiting.

Sebastian became distracted by something else as he watched Eleanor turning the cards over.

'Where did you get that pendant from?' He sounded more accusatory than he'd meant to.

Eleanor stopped what she was doing and reached for the sea-green stone.

'I can't really remember . . . I've had it for years. A craft shop near the coast I think. Unusual, isn't it?' She continued turning the cards over, unveiling the strange pictures.

'My mother had one just like it, same markings too, as I remember.' Sebastian felt confused; he was racking his brains to remember if his mother had been wearing it the last time he'd seen her. Then he recalled that last time, on the kitchen floor. He'd bent down to look at her under the table, the long silver chain had been draped across the base of her neck, the pendant lying on the floor near her ear lobe. The necklace he'd associated with his mother since he could remember.

All the time they were children, they'd been fascinated by the unusual wavy stripes of dark green and pale sea-blue polished stone that always reminded them of candy rock from the fair-ground. The memory punched him in the gut, he hadn't realised how much he missed her until now.

Eleanor gathered the cards from the table and began to shuffle them. She tapped the deck and handed the cards to Sebastian.

'Shuffle them.'

'No thanks, I need to get this coursework done.'

'There is always time for everything that's presented to us.' She thrust the deck towards him, taking the choice away.

Sighing, he shuffled the cards and handed them back to Eleanor, where she laid them on the table face down and began to peel each one from the top, laying them face up.

Silence descended like a misty spray as he waited for her to speak, to inform him of some doom ahead, or an amazing event that would astound him, but she didn't, her face barely altered from her usual expression. She observed the pictures for a few moments, gathered the cards up and began shuffling them again.

'Aren't you going to tell me what you saw?'

Eleanor leant back in her chair, observing him with the same interested expression she used for everything.

'I didn't say I was going to read your cards, I just asked you to shuffle them.'

'OK, but I'm interested to know what you saw.'

'Whatever I saw, you know already. You're just having trouble plucking it from your subconscious. But you will. Eventually.'

Sebastian stared at her for a few moments. 'Very cryptic.'

It was like a slap around the face. Sebastian felt the sting, and realised once again why it was that he didn't particularly like Eleanor or Samuel. They were subtly spiteful – subtle enough for most not to notice. Cecelia would tell him he was analysing things too deeply, that he'd taken it all the wrong way because he'd made the decision not to like Eleanor or Samuel. But he knew differently.

'I don't need to prove myself to you, Sebastian. My tarot is for my own interest.'

'Did you leave the newspaper on my bed?'

'Why does it matter who left the newspaper in your room? Information is delivered to us in all sorts of ways.' She set her light blue eyes on his face.

Sebastian knew he should walk away but his ego was tugging at him, the draught rising, making him want to see her beautiful skull crack on the hard stone floor.

14

Cecelia jiggled the bent hairpin in the lock and rammed her shoulder up against the door.

'The lock is jammed!' she hissed at Sebastian, who was busy trying to find another way in.

'This window is on the latch. I just need something to poke through and release it . . .'

'Can you stop messing about and shine the torch this way? I can't see what I'm doing,' Cecelia snapped. It was beginning to rain and she wanted to get inside, find what she was looking for and get out.

'Move over, let me try.'

'Why do you think you can do any better than me?' Cecelia stepped backwards.

'It would be quicker to break in,' Sebastian said to the sound of breaking glass against his elbow.

'What did you do that for?!'

'Who cares? It belongs to us now anyway . . .'

'You'd better sell a bit more on that stupid market stall to pay for that window pane.'

'You're a pain. What are we actually looking for?' Sebastian pulled himself into the dining room, quickly followed by Cecelia, who fell into him. They were both slightly merry, having been to one of the pubs in town to celebrate their sixteenth birthday. They'd told Eleanor they were going for fish and chips but Sebastian had talked Cecelia into having a few drinks beforehand. It was getting dark and they would be in trouble.

'You know the loft space in my bedroom where we used to sit?'

'Yeah . . .'

'Just after Mum went missing I was in there and I can't be sure of it but I think I saw a green suitcase resting on the beam, right at the far end. It's bugged me ever since and the discovery of that body in the woods has made me worry about it again.'

'Why?' Sebastian asked, holding her upright. 'I thought you said you knew who it was?'

'What if it was just gossip? I feel really pissed.' Cecelia was straining to see his face in the dark room, but she didn't want to switch the torch on and look at him.

'I think Roger might have put Mum's body in the suitcase . . .' She realised how silly it sounded once she'd said it out loud and she began to snigger and giggle.

Sebastian laughed even harder. 'Don't be ridiculous!'

Cecelia stopped giggling and glared at him, suddenly not finding any of it funny anymore.

'How the hell would he have fitted a body in a suitcase?' Sebastian's laughter was subsiding.

'I'm not going to answer that. Use your imagination.'

There was something different about Sebastian. She couldn't help feeling he knew something she didn't. He had a smug air about him, an arrogance she hadn't noticed before. He was dismissive, unavailable to her and she didn't like it. When Lola went to stay with her father, something she did every other weekend, Sebastian would sleep in Cecelia's room with her. The twins would curl up together as they always had at the farm, but recently, even though he was present physically, he was somehow absent.

'Stop taking the piss, Cece. We are not going into that loft space to drag out some old suitcase. We'll probably fall through the ceiling before finding it's been empty all along. And anyway, if Mum's body is in there, we do not need it to appear. Remember?'

'We need to look in the suitcase because if Mum's body is in there, we need to bury her somewhere before anyone else finds it. The discovery of it could still be dangerous for us. When the police have finished searching the area where the body was found, they'll come looking around the farm again for evidence. They've already said that woman died in suspicious circumstances. And once they start looking around the farm it doesn't take a genius to work out that there was once a door behind Roger's DIY efforts. This house will be torn apart. Do you see what I'm getting at, dear brother? If they *did* find Mum's body in the suitcase they might work out that she was dead before Roger and therefore can't have killed him.'

'Do you remember when you used to lose your voice more often . . . I preferred your silences.' Sebastian smirked at her as she held the bright torch in his face, his joke falling flat.

'What is wrong with you? You've been a right arsehole the last few days.'

'Nothing's wrong. Nothing . . . I'm fine, sorry.' He reached out to grab her, pull her towards him.

'Don't. I need to get on with this. If you can't take it seriously, piss off home.'

'Home?! That's a joke.'

'Stop feeling sorry for yourself!' Cecelia hissed at him in the darkness of the cold room. 'You don't like it there, I get it, but what do you want me to do about it? It's all we've got at the moment. And actually, I think it's all right. It's better than this place ever was, anyway.'

'I know. I just don't feel as close to you as I did before we lived there.'

Cecelia pulled him towards her sharply and kissed him on the cheek. 'You're so fucking needy. We're fine. Nothing's changed. Now let's get upstairs, this room gives me the creeps.'

Sebastian followed her through the rooms and up the back stairs in the kitchen that led to her bedroom. They had avoided the main staircase, not wanting to be reminded of what happened with Roger. They walked in silence and Cecelia was glad for the peace. She wanted to think, to clear her mind.

Upon entering her old bedroom, Cecelia drew in a sharp breath. It was the only room in the house that evoked a mixture of feelings.

'You OK, Mouse?'

'Yep, let's just get on with this.' Cecelia began to kick at the plasterboard. She'd expected it to cave in with very little force.

'You haven't really thought this through, have you?' Sebastian sat down on her old bed.

Cecelia looked at him as if he was stupid and turned her attention back to awkwardly bashing the wall with her foot.

'You could help?'

'Do you know how ridiculous this all sounds? Have you actually listened to what you're saying? Roger has *not* put our mother in a green suitcase. She'll be buried somewhere.'

'Sebastian, we both know she's dead. Why would a green suitcase suddenly appear? I'd never seen it before and then it appeared the day after Mum disappeared,' Cecelia said, breathing heavily from kicking the wall, hands on her hips.

'Maybe you just didn't notice it before. Cece . . .' Sebastian stood up from the bed and moved towards her. 'I need to tell you something.'

'What?'

Sebastian pulled her towards the bed where she sat down next to him.

'The day that Mum went missing . . . the day she left . . . I was here. I heard a gunshot. I saw her.'

Cecelia stared at him in the half-light, her eyes flickering from side to side as she concentrated on what he was saying.

'I don't understand. What do you mean you saw her? What, being shot? Dead?'

Sebastian shifted uncomfortably on the bed, making Cecelia move a few inches away from him so she could look at his face. The moon was offering a dim light through the window, splitting his face perfectly in two parts, so one half was completely blacked out in a symmetrical silhouette.

'When I came in from the farm, she was lying under the kitchen table.'

Cecelia looked puzzled. 'How did she get there?'

Sebastian frowned. 'I don't know, do I? What does that matter anyway?'

'Let's just get on with finding that case.' Cecelia got up from her bed and began ferociously kicking the plasterboard where a hole had already appeared. It wasn't until she paused briefly, did she realise Sebastian was trying to talk to her.

'Cece, what are you doing?'

'You're becoming really tiresome now, Sebastian.'

'I've just told you I saw our mother dead on the kitchen floor and you've barely said anything.'

'What is there to say? It doesn't change anything, doesn't alter our situation. We don't need the body of our mother to be found, wherever she is. We've told the police she killed our father and fled the farm.' Cecelia faced the dark room and the mess she'd made, not wanting him to see she was crying. 'I knew she was dead, I told you that at the time.'

The missing suitcase, Roger, the dead woman in the copse, it was all too much for Cecelia. She stepped forward and hit Sebastian hard in the face. As soon as she'd done it, she regretted it, throwing herself at him as she had at Lola.

'I'm so sorry, I'm so sorry,' she cried into his chest.

'It's OK, Cece, it's OK. Everything is going to be OK.' He kissed her head and stroked her hair.

Cecelia reached up and gently touched his cheek where she'd hit him. Sebastian moved round and kissed her hand, her face – she could smell the sweet alcohol on his breath. She pulled away from him so she could see the familiarity in his eyes, but her thoughts were interrupted by those of Samuel. Sebastian placed his hand on her jaw, tracing the line of her lips with his thumb. Sudden movement from downstairs startled them both.

'What was that?' Cecelia whispered.

'Shush . . .'

The door to the kitchen stairs creaked open. Cecelia gripped hold of Sebastian as they both held their breath, feet stuck to the floor, hearts pounding.

'Hello?' A voice called from halfway up the staircase. They stayed absolutely still and silent by the window, neither of them daring to move. The voice sounded again, clearer this time.

'Shit!' Sebastian whispered louder than he'd meant to. 'That was . . . that was . . .'

Lights they didn't even know worked suddenly flooded the hallway.

'What's going on?'

Cecelia pulled herself away from Sebastian to see Yvonne standing in the doorway of her bedroom.

15

Sebastian wanted to stay at the foster house, regardless of how he felt about the place. The alternative – going back to White Horse Farm – wasn't something he would ever want to do. He'd been asked whether he wanted to go and live with his mother again, as had Cecelia. Both of them had refused to answer and Cecelia had said she would stay with him wherever he went. He hadn't been entirely convinced by her words. There had been a strange atmosphere between Cecelia and Yvonne, something he couldn't understand. It hadn't been anything either of them had said, but there was something underlying their words.

Now Sebastian was faced with another dilemma. The police had been searching for their mother because he and Cecelia had suggested she'd killed Roger. They wouldn't have done this if they hadn't thought she was dead. Now the police would be trying to find out who had killed Roger.

When they had recovered from the shock of seeing Yvonne, there had been no hugs or embraces and there was a complete lack of warmth from Yvonne, or Cecelia, for that matter. He'd found it so strange that Cecelia hadn't sought it from her, he knew how close they'd been.

'But I saw you under the table,' Sebastian had said to his mother churlishly. 'I saw you dead.'

'Obviously not, son.' Yvonne lit a cigarette as they sat in the sitting room talking. 'Your father and I had just had an argument. I'd had a bit to drink and I fell over and smacked my head.'

Sebastian nodded. He hadn't known what to say. His mother seemed different. Not the same, soft person he remembered. Yvonne had been replaced by someone matter of fact, cold and hard, and even her face had a sharp edge he didn't recall seeing before.

'You've been gone for more than a year,' Cecelia blurted out, staring at the table, rubbing the dent in the veneer as she always had done.

'Well, I'm back now. I've been staying with a friend.'

'A friend?' Sebastian couldn't believe what he was hearing. 'Where?'

'A long way from here . . . I wasn't in a good place . . . we thought it was for the best, your father and I. When I got myself together, he drove me over there and told me never to contact any of you ever again.'

'So Dad was telling the truth,' said Sebastian.

'We thought you were dead,' Cecelia kept saying over and over again, making him want to smack the side of her head.

'You haven't even called us. Not once.'

'I did, but there was never any answer . . . like I said, I haven't been in a good place. Anyway, it's not the first time I've gone away . . . you mice know what your old Mum's like.' She smiled half-heartedly. 'Where's your father?'

'We thought you were dead,' Cecelia whispered, pulling her knees up to her chest, hugging her legs.

'You've been gone all this time? Not been back at all?' said Sebastian.

'No son . . . as I said, I have gone away before . . .' He could see Yvonne's guilt was finally rising to the surface as it dawned on her what day it was. She'd never missed their birthdays, however many times she'd left them.

'I know, but not for this long.'

'You're supposed to be dead.'

'Yes, Cecelia, we thought she was dead,' Sebastian said sarcastically, not really registering her choice of words.

'I bet you did. I suppose your father told you that? He obviously didn't give you my letters. Where is he? I came here earlier and couldn't find him anywhere.'

'He's dead.' Sebastian spat the words across the table keeping his eyes on his sister.

'And we told the police you did it . . .' Cecelia blurted, laughter erupting from her as though she was being sick.

Sebastian watched her stifling the noise into her knees as she gently rocked backwards and forwards on the chair.

16

The shock of her mother returning triggered another night-mare which caused Cecelia's voice to disappear once again, rather in the same way Yvonne had vanished. She had thought she'd never see her again, the memories of that day scorched on her brain. She'd grieved for this woman, felt the pain of her absence and, somehow, she now didn't want her back. Not this version of her mother anyway. Wherever she'd been the past year, whoever she'd been with, had chiselled her into someone quite selfish.

Devoid of any words that made sense to her, Cecelia slipped back into her own private world, somewhere so deep that even Sebastian couldn't enter. She preferred it like that, silent conversations she played in her mind; words no one else could hear unless they were uttered, made her feel safe. Sometimes she made entire conversations up with people in her mind, occasionally allowing herself to replay real ones, as though she had stored them on file in a library set up in her head. Lola, for all her nervous chatter, was a pleasant distraction, and had relaxed more in her company, although she occasionally treated her as though she was deaf rather than mute and raised her voice higher than necessary. It was a mistake lots of people made when they saw Cecelia and Sebastian signing to one another.

The days running up to their arrest had passed slowly, even though they were busy with exams and studying. They realised that once the police had spoken to Yvonne and discovered that she had an alibi for the time of Roger's murder, they would start looking to Cecelia and Sebastian for answers.

It was a Saturday morning – they'd both been agitated, pacing up and down the loft room, looking out of the window, then at the clock on the bedside table. Sebastian had tried to draw Cecelia but he couldn't concentrate and screwed-up sketch paper littered the floor.

Cecelia had pointed at the linen etchings that he'd hung up from string in the loft room and signed to him that they should take them down.

'No, Cece! It doesn't mean anything, it's just art.'

For me, she'd signed to him, placing her hand on her chest. She was worried about what it would look like to the police. They would think it was weird. Cecelia was convinced that if they played everything down, no one would suspect anything. It was naive and showed the child that was still present within her. Turning sixteen didn't automatically make you an adult, she realised that now.

They were both taken in for questioning that day, a sign language expert brought in on Cecelia's behalf. Her voice was safely away somewhere, unable to harm her. She hadn't protested at all when Eleanor had picked her up later that night and taken her home, leaving Sebastian at the police station. That's what he'd have wanted, she was sure of it. He'd answer the police questions and would sort everything out. Then Eleanor told her the next day that Sebastian was being charged with murder. And still she did nothing, said nothing, didn't tell anyone that Sebastian was innocent and that she was the guilty one.

Not even when Eleanor told her Samuel was preparing Roger's funeral, his body having been released. Before she knew it, Cecelia found herself standing opposite her mother, Roger's coffin separating them. A wave of Sebastian's absence hit her and she began to sob quietly, the mourners thinking her tears were for Roger.

Cecelia's insides turned whenever Yvonne caught her looking at her and she turned her glance away, but her mother hooked her eyesight a little longer each time. She'd been dreading the day of the funeral, particularly without Sebastian by her side. He had been granted permission to attend but had refused. Cecelia now regretted her feelings of the past few weeks when she'd wanted to distance herself from Sebastian and feel more independent.

'Can I have a word, Cece?' Yvonne caught up with her before she could scamper into the car with her foster mother.

'Two minutes,' Eleanor said to Yvonne.

'Don't tell me how much time I can have with my daughter.'

Eleanor ignored her and made her way to the car park with Samuel.

'Do you want to come back to the farm with me? I can make that happen, if you'd like?'

Cecelia shook her head, uncomfortable at her mother's close proximity to her, her face so near she could smell the mix of nicotine and cheap mints on her breath. She moved to walk away but Yvonne grabbed her arm.

'Think about it and let me know. It would be like we always planned, remember? Just think about it. For me, Cece.'

Cecelia shrugged, looking up to see Eleanor pulling the car up the road to meet her, check she was OK.

'Think about it,' her mother said again, more forcefully.

Cecelia nodded, turning to walk away, agreeing just so she could leave.

'I haven't forgotten what you did.'

Stopping in her tracks Cecelia turned back slowly and looked at Yvonne.

'I wouldn't ever forget something like that, Mouse, not ever.'

That was the answer to the question Cecelia had been desperate to ask ever since her mother had come back. But she hadn't been able to work out how to ask someone if they remembered you'd tried to kill them.

PART 2

18 YEARS LATER

1

After Sebastian's release from prison, he spent a few weeks in accommodation arranged by his probation officer. It wasn't ideal. It was a flat in the middle of his home town – the usual concrete block soaked in piss – a dumping ground for rubbish with an acrid odour on the stairs and in the corridors that permeated his flat. Even the flat wasn't much better, with soiled carpets and a constant ghost of a smell he couldn't erase, reminding him of the bottom of a rancid waste bin.

Today he was standing outside a terraced house with the same bin liner of items he'd left prison with. He looked down at a small scrap of paper in his hand, checking the address that was written in pencil, making sure he'd knocked on the correct door. The house belonged to his mother. She'd come to see him at the flat and had been so shocked by its state that she'd promptly asked him to move in with her. Sebastian wasn't sure how it was all going to work out but he was grateful for the offer, which came complete with her company and support.

Yvonne had continued to visit Sebastian throughout his time in prison. They'd never been entirely comfortable with one another, mainly passing small talk back and forth across the table. In prison, he'd followed a strict routine and the only topics of conversation he could offer were his studies and the interesting courses he was covering, which he gulped down to alleviate the boredom. In return, she told him of trivial matters that were of no interest to him, as though she was trying to avoid discussing anything meaningful.

An example of her avoiding such discussion was the house Sebastian stood in front of now. An inheritance from Yvonne's mother, who had died when Sebastian and Cecelia were small. Yvonne had rented it out for many years, giving her an income that she'd saved and hidden from Roger. Sebastian had wanted to ask why they hadn't left the farm before. Eighteen years of his life might have been saved had they not stayed with Roger for all those years. But it didn't need to be said; it hung in the air between them, along with lots of other questions that were all strung along the invisible washing line.

'Come in, son,' said Yvonne when she had eventually opened the door. He was beginning to wonder if she'd changed her mind.

Sebastian stepped into a fairly cluttered room. An uncomfortable looking two-seater sofa with wooden arms sat in front of an old gas fire. The rest of the space was taken up with glass cabinets full of ornaments which rattled when he walked past. A small dark hallway beyond revealed a steep staircase that his mother had already begun to ascend.

'I'll show you up here first, then we'll have a cup of tea. Did you get the bus?'

'No, I walked. Needed the fresh air. It's still a novelty.'

Yvonne laughed harder than the joke warranted.

'Are you sure this is OK, Mum?'

'Yes, son. You'll have to pay me some rent once you get yourself a job though.'

'Sure.' Sebastian recalled the conversation he'd had with his probation officer about helping him with job applications. When Sebastian had mentioned taking up his market stall again, making some money that way, as well as pursuing his art, a faint knowing smile had appeared on the man's lips and he'd continued his lecture about jobs and what would be achievable for Sebastian at that time. These people knew how to crush the life out of you and he had made a mental note to be less forthcoming in future.

'No funny business though . . . know what I mean?'

They'd reached the landing where they were surrounded by three entrances. The one directly in front of them led to the largest room which contained a bathroom, and there were smaller rooms to the left and right.

'Funny business, Mother? I've just spent more than half my life locked up.'

'I know, son.' Yvonne reached behind her and squeezed his arm, but he noticed she couldn't look him in the eyes.

They were stood in the largest room; a double bed seemed lost against the back wall. It was basic – empty and old fashioned – but Sebastian found it light relief from the clutter of downstairs.

'You can have this floor to yourself. I sleep in the basement. I had it converted into two bedrooms and a bathroom a few years ago so I could have a lodger up here. We'll share the kitchen and living room of course, although one of these rooms does have armchairs in it as well.'

'It's nice ...' Sebastian hadn't expected an entire floor to himself – something else Yvonne hadn't mentioned before.

'The tenant has only just left, that's why I haven't ...' She tailed off, reading his mind, wanting him to fill in the blank spaces, smother her guilt, tell her it was OK, but he didn't.

Downstairs there was another sitting room, larger than the first and just by the door to the kitchen stood a fold-down dining table and chairs. Instead of glass cabinets full of ornaments, there were small occasional tables piled with cut outs from magazines – recipes, knitting patterns, various articles – and the dusty television was weighted with folded sections of newspapers. A familiar feeling rose in Sebastian's stomach as, unused to clutter, he was beginning to feel closed in. He pulled a pouch of tobacco from his back pocket and began rolling a cigarette to distract himself. Pushing past his mother in the galley kitchen he found his way into the small back garden.

'You all right?' Yvonne called.

'Yes, fine. Don't like being shut in for too long.'

She laughed inappropriately again. 'I should think they all say that.'

'I'm sure "they" do,' Sebastian said, frowning.

He looked up at the tall buildings – a long row of almost identical terraces apart from the various coloured window frames and items of clothing draped from washing lines hanging high in the air. He turned to see a woman's face peering out from behind an old net curtain in an upstairs window. She glared at him disapprovingly.

'Don't take any notice of her. That's Mrs Dalton; nosy old bag she is.' Yvonne handed him a mug of strong tea.

'What have you done to your hair, Mum?'

'Do you like it? I thought I'd have a change.' She touched the back of her French pleat with her red varnished nails.

'Nice. You look good.' Sebastian observed her, saw the prettiness of her flecked green eyes, the gentle dip of the sockets which led to the soft ascension of her cheeks. She was more vibrant than when she'd been with Roger all those years ago. Now he was viewing her in colour and he'd only just noticed it.

'Have you thought about what you're going to do for work?' Yvonne balanced her cup on an old plant pot and lit her own cigarette.

'Do you know many people who want to employ someone with a criminal record?'

'Some people must do, love. You're not the only one out there.'

'I've been helping out on the market stalls, putting a bit of cash away so I can set up on my own. I used to sell gloves and socks, waterproof gear – did quite well at it. I can keep my head down that way.' He didn't tell her he planned to exhibit some of his artwork. After the reaction he got from his probation officer, he thought it was best to keep it to himself.

'That's a good idea. I could help you get set up, lend you some cash?'

'No thanks, Mum; I want to do this on my own. I'm selling quite a lot for the stall holders and they're giving me a good cut. It won't take me long. They don't remember what happened . . . and no questions are asked, which is fine by me.'

'Got your father's gob, I suppose. He'd have made a good salesman, if he hadn't been so uptight . . .'

The mention of Roger turned the atmosphere sour and Sebastian went back indoors and poured himself a fresh cup of tea, which he drank quickly.

'Anything you want me to get? I'm going into town,' asked Sebastian, as he ran back upstairs to get his coat and survey his new surroundings, calculating what he might need to buy in the coming weeks. Although there was plenty of furniture, it was a bit stark. It really needed some paint and pictures. There was a strange collage covering one of the walls in the smallest bedroom made up of little pieces of carefully cut sentences and words that had been glued on in straight lines, so that one word followed the next, stringing together sentences that didn't make sense. Sebastian moved closer and began to read the hundreds of words that covered the wall. It all looked so familiar to him. And then he remembered Cecelia snipping sections out of old books, sentences she particularly liked – such was her obsession with words.

'Has Cecelia stayed here?' he asked Yvonne once he was back downstairs.

'I've got some letters I'd like you to post. Oh, and could you pick up something for supper, I'll give you the money.'

'Mum?'

'Yes, son. She stayed here for a few months when Caroline was about ten. She needed time apart from Samuel. They'd been through a bad patch. . .'

'Caroline?'

'Yes, Caroline. Your niece.'

'A few months? And you never told me?'

'Yes. And no, I didn't.' Yvonne was becoming agitated at his questioning.

'Caroline . . .' Sebastian tried the name quietly.

'I haven't seen her for years, not to speak to anyway, just the odd glimpse outside the school when she was younger. I've seen her working in Cecelia's bookshop recently. She must be seventeen or eighteen by now.'

'I didn't know Cecelia owned a bookshop.'

'Why would you?' Yvonne said, a little too abruptly. 'On King's Street, it is. I sit in the café opposite sometimes, just people watching.' Yvonne distracted herself with a search through her address book.

'How come you don't see them anymore?'

'It didn't work out, that's all,' she finally said.

'What's going on, Mum?'

The sudden bang of Yvonne's fist on the precarious dining table made Sebastian flinch. Without looking at him, she got up from where she was sitting and went downstairs to her basement.

When Sebastian arrived back from town she was asleep on the sofa, make-up smudged across her face and her hair in a knotted mess on the cushion.

2

Through the kitchen window, across the long back garden and amidst all the people, Cecelia could see a man standing at the small side gate. He was framed by the honeysuckle-covered arch; the orange sky in the distance was burning a warm glow across all the shapes it touched. Just within reach of her vision she could see the tip of a silver blade poking out from behind the jug and the coffee pot where she'd tried to conceal it. The scene before her was much more sinister and foreboding than it should have been. It was not something she'd expected to see during her daughter's seventeenth birthday party. And she knew that through the haze of people and the noise, that he could see her just as much as she could see him. Despite the differences in his matured face, she could see the unmistakable ghost of Sebastian as a boy.

It had been seventeen years since she'd seen him last. She'd supported him during the run-up to his trial, feeling it was the least she could do since she'd been somewhat to blame for his incarceration. But then their relationship had begun to corrode – he was bitter and angry, but said he didn't blame her for what had happened. After a few months she realised she couldn't face him anymore. They had both thought their mother would shoulder the blame, state the part she had played which had led to the shooting of Roger. But neither of them had told Yvonne which one of them had killed Roger and so she'd just assumed it was Sebastian who had done it. Sebastian wanted to take the blame, he was protecting Cecelia and she had allowed him to, naively thinking that would be the last of it.

After Sebastian had been sentenced, Cecelia had turned to Samuel in his absence. Any talk of him during Cecelia's visits to the young offender's unit just fuelled a temper in Sebastian that she hadn't seen before. Once she'd told him she was expecting a baby with Samuel, Sebastian had refused to see her. Around their eighteenth birthdays, she heard that he'd been moved to an adult prison to serve the rest of his sentence. Somehow, through all the lies and false statements, she'd convinced herself that she was innocent, passing opinion about the situation when it arose between those around her as though she couldn't believe her brother was capable of murder, as if she was as shocked as they were.

Some months later, childbirth had engulfed her. She had been so young at eighteen, and her time had been taken over by new life, and the separation from Sebastian made her realise how unhealthy their relationship had been. The longer she stayed away, the easier it was to never go back.

And here Sebastian was now, at her gate, where she'd seen him regularly over the past two weeks. It was the same place they'd last lived together, their foster home, which had become Cecelia's permanent residence after she'd married Samuel.

She'd spent the last few years questioning her reasons for this decision.

Sebastian didn't venture beyond the garden boundary, and she in turn never went out to him. It was clear that they wanted to meet, but neither one acted on the impulse.

The day that Sebastian had been convicted, one of the foster children who had been there less than a week took himself down to the war bunker and slit his wrists. He survived but the whole incident was seen as a bad omen. From then on their home, her sanctuary, was strictly void of anything she deemed foreboding or sinister. There had been enough horrible things leaking through the cracks in the walls throughout her childhood.

Sebastian's release from prison coincided with the discovery of the blasted knife and Cecelia couldn't help feeling it was symbolic. The knife she couldn't bring herself to dispose of for fear of it bleeding a curse over her family – a superstition that she had picked up from Eleanor. There was something about this particular knife. It was long with an arched blade decorated with an engraved pattern on one side of the handle, which was now worn and looked like an old piece of driftwood. She couldn't bear to touch it, and even briefly resting on what it might have been used for and why it had been concealed in the back of a drawer caused her nerves to shudder, her imagination running wild. The old house didn't help disperse the feeling that something bad would happen if they got rid of it. Now she just wished Samuel hadn't shown it to her. He'd bought an old chest from an antique place around the corner, and upon pulling out the drawers in order to fit it into the back of the car, he had found it bumping around inside. Why had he brought it home, was all she kept thinking. If only he'd disposed of it on his way back. She was angry that he hadn't had any forethought or understanding.

So, for fear that she'd be cursed if she got rid of it, Cecelia placed it on the kitchen window sill behind some old jugs, where it couldn't be seen, but it was an acknowledgement to her superstition that she'd actually given it a home. From then on, it tormented her with its presence. She was worried that one of her family might find it and hurt themselves or someone else, or that she might do something with it during one of her sleepwalking episodes, which had become more frequent of late.

In the end, Samuel had come up with the idea to bury it – that way, they were keeping it, but it was away from the house. She was glad to pass the burden to him, relinquishing all responsibility for the consequences. She'd completely ignored the fact she'd been an accessory to the crime, having watched the burial of it from the gentle confines of her home. And then, shortly afterwards, she'd dug it up during the night, washed it and placed it back on the window sill. Although she had no recollection of doing it, the muddy evidence was caked beneath her nails. But there had been some comfort in having it back in the house. It was a feeling she couldn't explain – that maybe facing her fears would disperse them in some way.

For a while she'd felt greatly relieved and then the wind picked up, carrying the leaves across the garden like snowfall, and everything had changed.

Sebastian's presence today was different. She'd felt something pulling her towards him like she always had before he went away, but this was slightly different as Sebastian wasn't facing her. She followed his gaze and saw her daughter, Caroline, talking to some of her friends. Sebastian watching her intently. Her beautiful Caroline.

Swilling the shards of ice in her drink, she drained the rest of the vodka in her glass. When she looked back, he'd gone. The tip of the blade on the window sill seemed more prominent than ever as it glistened in the shine of the twinkling garden lights hanging from the window. Her obsession with that knife hadn't just been a coincidence; it had appeared in her life for a reason.

3

Sebastian squirted several different coloured oils onto his make-shift easel – a large piece of board he'd found in the cupboard under the stairs. Emptying each tube, he took his palette knife and began scraping up the paint and swirling it onto the main wall of the loft room. It had taken him an entire day to remove all the pieces of paper Cecelia had pasted onto the wall all those years ago. The varying shapes and italics had irritated him some-what; it was a confusion of shapes, lines and dirty shades of white, completely unfitting for his idea of art. It occurred to him how typical it was of Cecelia to be so flippant with the layout, and, so it appeared, in most things in her life.

Standing back, he observed the rough pencil outline of what he wanted the subject to look like. Now he could add plenty of colour, bringing the abstract face to life. She was a prison officer he'd been mildly infatuated with. No one understood that it was her face, her frame he was most interested in; she had an incred-ible balance that ran through her entire being. The images of her had never left his mind and, until he recreated her in oils, the emotions he felt would never subside. She'd been his friend to begin with, or so he'd thought, and he knew he hadn't imagined the odd glance, or the way she singled him out with a touch on the arm, a squeeze of his shoulder. In the end she'd transferred to a new wing.

Sebastian's creative surge lasted for most of the day and it filled him with a deep satisfaction to let go of the erotic images he'd been carrying around in his head. She was beautiful, but only he would know who was painted on the wall, and that alone thrilled him.

Sitting down on the sofa, he lit a cigarette and looked up at the face that was indecipherable to anyone but him. Resting the cigarette in the glass ashtray on the coffee table he placed his hands together, finger to finger, perfectly matching. It offered some calm relief, eased the draught that seemed to be permanently hovering in the bottom of his stomach. He closed his eyes, smoke swirled around the ashtray and across the coffee table, visions of Cecelia merged with Caroline; the draught was lifting and he knew it was time for a walk. In prison he'd learnt that movement helped the draught to subside. It was far better than staying in the same place and losing his mind altogether. A psychologist's assessment told him he was suffering from anxiety but he wasn't convinced of this diagnosis.

'Just going for a walk,' he called to Yvonne, who was in the kitchen cooking.

'OK. You haven't forgotten I'm going out, have you?'

'Nope. See you later.'

It was dusk, his favourite time for wandering. There was always a whisper of anticipation in the air, an expectation that everything could suddenly change under the night's dark shadow.

On his way back he stopped at the shop around the corner from his house to pick up some newspapers and cigarettes. The only publications available in prison were tabloids that were shared around and that he didn't really care for. The lack of reading material and Sebastian's extreme boredom had caused another slight obsession to develop and now, free of any restrictions, he took great pleasure in buying several broadsheets every day. There wasn't always time to read everything, but knowing he had been free to purchase them was enough.

Before he let himself into Yvonne's house he paused on the opposite side of the road, observing the orange-lit street and the place he now lived. A house he was now seeing differently since finding out that Cecelia had lived there, albeit briefly.

Glancing up, he saw a young woman staring at him from the upstairs window of the house two doors down. She was pretty in a flat, uncharismatic way, but there was something oddly familiar about her. He knew her large dark eyes from somewhere. He noticed her hair was parted to the left side, with the rest tied in a ponytail loosely hanging on her right shoulder. The draught lifted slightly in the bottom of his stomach, the lack of symmetry beginning to bother him.

The woman smiled and hesitantly lifted her hand in a gesture of greeting. He stared at her for a few moments, as her fingers crumpled like paper back down to her side, and then he crossed the street and went inside his house.

Pouring himself a glass of wine he observed the woman he'd seen at the window in his mind, registering his presumed facts about her as he did with anyone he focused on for any length of time: drab shirt, one size too big, worn out bra, one breast hanging irritatingly lower than the other. He imagined her to have a small amount of make-up layered on top of the previous day's. Not enough to show that she'd made an effort – further evidence of a lack of interest in herself and suggesting low confidence.

Glancing at the window, his eyes focusing, he caught a glimpse of his own face, the stark kitchen light shining above his head projecting two reflections. He might have appeared saintly if it hadn't been for the slight expression of disgust he was unaware of. He despised people like her: lazy, pathetic and unkempt. Not like Cecelia.

Taking his wine and freshly rolled cigarettes into the sitting room he began to carefully look through the broadsheets, before folding and adding them to the new pile which was growing like an arch of thorny roses either side of the door to the understairs cupboard. He was adding some balanced order to his mother's clutter.

Stoking the fire for the night, he made his way up to the bathroom and began filling the tub. For the first time in over eighteen years he was going to sit in the bath and draw. He paused in the doorway, remembering Cecelia sitting on the old wooden chair, allowing him to draw her as she chatted. The rickety old chair had been her favourite seat in the old farmhouse. Now, in the bigger picture he held in his mind, Caroline was sitting there instead.

Shutting off the taps he walked into the room where he'd been painting and sat down to observe his work from a new perspective.

Closing his eyes he visualised Caroline, his mind settling on the symmetry of her face, the definition of her straight, freckled nose, blunt cut fringe and long hair. Her cheekbones were still developing underneath her flesh. Flesh that would thin as the years passed, revealing two beautifully carved bones, identical to her mother's.

In the bath he occupied himself drawing Caroline's perfect, almond-shaped green eyes. Like the old days, he thought. It would be just like the old days.

4

The blade of the knife winked at Cecelia from its place on the window sill. She took a deep breath and counted, one . . . two . . . three . . . four. Sebastian was at the gate again, like a dark apparition hovering outside their home, threatening to upturn her family like broken furniture.

'Who is that man at the gate?' Caroline stood up from the kitchen table to get a better look. 'I've seen him before.'

'Have you?' Cecelia was wistful, not really present within the room. She was strangely drawn to Sebastian and had found herself looking out for him each day, however much she told herself she didn't want to see him or allow him to be a part of her life, the pull was there – the same connection they'd had to one another when they were children.

'Yeah, he's been hanging around outside the school . . . always smiles at me . . . like he knows me. Bit weird.'

'He does what outside the school?' Cecelia landed back in the room with a thud.

Caroline tutted. 'I just said, I've seen him outside the school. He looks at me like he knows me . . . Who is he, Mum? Do you know him? He looks ever so much like you. He's not a long lost relative is he?!' She laughed, pushing her chair back as she packed away her school books.

'You haven't spoken to him, have you?' Cecelia grabbed Caroline's arm.

'No! Why?' Caroline tried to pull away.

'Because . . . I don't want you to.' Cecelia released her fingers, and it was only then that she realised how hard she'd been gripping her daughter's arm.

They held each other's gaze.

'Tell me why first.'

'You shouldn't need a reason why, you should just do as I ask.'

'Oh come on, Mum, who is he? If you don't tell me, I'll just get it out of Dad.'

Cecelia pulled out a chair and sat down at the table. 'He's my brother . . . My twin, actually . . .'

A cold silence drifted through the kitchen and Cecelia looked up to see an open-mouthed Caroline. Her face so quickly becoming child-like, as it always did when she was upset. Cecelia missed that little girl; she'd begun to feel her slipping away rapidly when she'd reached seventeen. She watched Caroline fall rather than sit back down in her chair. Then the rubble began tumbling down the cliff as Cecelia realised the enormity of what she'd said.

'You're not a twin, you're lying . . .'

Cecelia sighed. 'I'm not lying; he is my twin brother, Sebastian.'

'Sebastian? You told me he was your uncle. Your uncle who shot your father.'

'No.' Cecelia shook her head. 'Sebastian is my brother, there is no uncle.'

'Your brother killed your dad?' The rims of Caroline's eyes were quickly turning red.

'That's why I don't want you having anything to do with him.' Cecelia decided to avoid Caroline's question, convincing herself she was telling the truth.

'How could you lie to me about something like that?' Caroline's lip trembled. 'You told me you were an only child ... how could you do that ... knowing I'm a twin as well ...'

'Caroline ...'

The chair tumbled backwards and before Cecelia could stop her, Caroline had run from the room, her footsteps resounding on the wooden staircase.

'What's wrong with her now?' Samuel wandered in from the sitting room, empty mug in his hand.

'I've just told her about Sebastian.' She sighed.

'What, all of it, or just about him being your brother?'

'All of it,' she said, with slight irritation.

Samuel placed his cup next to the kettle and switched it on.

'She was bound to find out some time. It's better it comes from you than from someone else. He's been released, for God's sake; you know how people talk, especially round here.'

'Yes, but it holds far more meaning for her, doesn't it?'

'I don't understand.'

'Yes you do. I told you this would happen and, as always, you refused to pay any attention.' Cecelia stood up, her chair rattling to steady itself as she roughly shoved it towards the table.

'This is ridiculous. You've told her you have a twin. Big deal. She's just being melodramatic, like all teenagers are. I would have thought she'd be more upset that he killed her grandfather.'

'Well, she knows how I felt about Roger, how he treated us, so she wouldn't be that bothered. She didn't even know him.'

'All beyond me. I can't understand why she gets so upset about everything.' Samuel peered into the fridge while he waited for the kettle to boil, assessing the food. 'What are we going to have for dinner?'

'Are you just pretending to be stupid?' She stared at him, waiting for the information to connect to his brain. 'I'm a twin, she's a twin.'

'Yes. There are lots of twins all over the world. I still don't see why finding out you're a twin has any consequence on her life. It really has nothing to do with her. She had a sister, not a brother, and don't give me all that crap about twins sharing a secret world that no one else understands.'

'But it has a huge impact on her life, Samuel, it really has . . . and actually, it's not crap, twins are part of a special relationship that no one else could ever begin to understand.' Cecelia shook her head at him and walked from the room. 'You especially,' she muttered under her breath. The words rested on her lips, then crept back in like small crabs, making her swallow hard as she felt them catch in her throat, threatening to choke her.

'Everything OK?' Eleanor looked up from her armchair as Cecelia walked into the garden room.

'Just the usual. Caroline's upset, Samuel doesn't understand.' She brushed it off with her hand, not wanting to burden her mother-in-law with anything negative; she was ill and didn't need to hear about their family troubles.

'Parts of my body might be giving up but there's nothing wrong with my eyes and ears. I've seen Sebastian hanging around.'

'It's nothing for you to worry about.' Cecelia absently flicked through a magazine, seeing the articles without registering them.

'When have I ever worried about anything? Maybe you should ask him in, leave the past behind.'

'Maybe you should keep your opinions to yourself.' As soon as Cecelia said it, she wished she could take it back.

Eleanor's eyebrows rose slightly. 'Sebastian is your twin brother; you were so close once. I remember the bond you had with one another.' She looked at Cecelia pointedly.

'What do you mean?' Cecelia put the magazine back on the coffee table and eyed Eleanor with interest.

'Just that. You were very close.'

'Yes, we were,' Cecelia snapped. 'Were being the operative word. I don't want him anywhere near Caroline.'

Eleanor began to cough. Her chest was now like a small brittle cage housing two little blackened birds. She still wore the same floaty clothes she'd always worn. They never covered her properly, even less so now her illness had really taken a grip on her body. When she coughed, Cecelia imagined she could see the cancer through her transparent skin.

'I've learnt something over the years, an old cliché but a good one: keep your enemies close, Cecelia. I always did.' Eleanor looked at Cecelia, her expression cold and hard.

'I need to check on Caroline and think about what we're all going to have for dinner.' Cecelia got up from her seat and went to leave the room, but Eleanor grabbed her arm on the way past.

'I know, Cecelia.'

Cecelia pulled her arm free from Eleanor's bony fingers. 'You don't know anything,' she hissed into her face.

5

When Sebastian stepped away from Yvonne's house – she'd gone away for a few days – he started thinking about their relationship. As far as Yvonne knew, Sebastian had killed Roger. They'd never talked about it when she visited him in prison and they had avoided the subject since he'd moved in, a kind of silent agreement between the two of them.

He'd fallen into a routine alongside her, a structure he quite enjoyed. After so many years of set boundaries, he'd been anxious about how he would conduct his life without instruction. Although now he had the added thrill of being able to make choices outside the rules if he wished to do so. Yvonne followed the same pattern each week, vehement that she didn't have any sort of routine because Monday was different to Tuesday, as was Wednesday, and so it went on until she reached the beginning of the week and it all started again.

Sebastian found this a calming influence, a gentle ease to his turbulent emotions and the feelings that had risen to the surface since he'd seen Cecelia. His probation officer said he'd feel unsettled – it was normal when you'd spent so many years in an institution. He said a lot of things, Sebastian's probation officer.

Sometimes it sounded like he was repeating the same sentences, as though every case was the same.

Pausing on the street corner, as he did every night when he collected the newspapers, Sebastian saw the woman who had waved from the window coming out of her front door. Once she was stood next to him he realised who she was. She was one of the weird twins that he and Cecelia had spent time with at the foster home; the 'gorgeous girls' as he and his friends had called them, their looks were so striking. He didn't know why he was so surprised she'd grown up. As he looked at her face he thought it was a shame. He wished he hadn't seen her again. She'd been so pretty back then and even though he knew this woman was definitely her, she didn't fit the person he had stored away in his memory.

'I thought I'd come and say hello rather than just waving from the window.'

'Hello,' Sebastian said, searching her face for the person he remembered, instead seeing the unfamiliar woman before him. 'You're one of the twins from the foster home?'

'That's right. I recognised you straightaway . . . you haven't changed at all.'

'Oh, I have,' Sebastian muttered, although, he thought, not in the ways she meant. He continued to stare at the house, the transition from inside to out having not yet ceased to fascinate him. 'I can't remember your names, which one are you?'

'Ava . . . Why do you always stop on the corner before you go in? I see you most evenings.'

Sebastian looked at her – she seemed taller, more elegant than when he'd seen her through the window and it was as though he was continuing a conversation with someone he knew well.

'Why do you stare out of the window every night?'

Ava frowned, unsure whether he was being friendly or sarcastic. He knew there was no point in giving her a proper answer as any explanation of his need to stand outside – experiencing freedom instead of confinement – would be lost on her. She chose to laugh off what he said.

'Do you fancy going for a drink?'

'What, now?' Sebastian suddenly became aware of his freedom again, a frequent occurrence since being released from prison.

'Yes . . .' Ava turned to stare at him squarely in the face, clearly expecting him to say no.

They chose a pub on the outskirts of town, a slightly stark place but bustling all the same. The conversation was awkward, clumsy to begin with, until after their first drink when Ava relaxed.

Sebastian pressed her for details about Cecelia and Samuel, assuming she'd know something about them since she'd stayed in the area. She wasn't forthcoming though, answering each of his questions with only one word. She was mildly interesting, but mainly boring, steering the conversation round to her work; she had qualified as an accountant but hadn't yet taken her official exams in order to be classed as chartered. He had no idea why this was as each time he asked the question, his mind wandered and the answer just wouldn't sink in. She only talked about her own life – a background drone of information he didn't particularly care about – until there was any mention of Cecelia, who she claimed to have been back in touch with. He was happy to listen, quite content to explore her from the top of her head downwards, taking in her lopsided shoulders and her breastbone, which he noticed was protruding slightly more on the left than the right. He wanted to rearrange her frame, mould it back into perfect form with his fingers. He liked the mixed sensations her imperfections gave him, the draught hovering dangerously near the surface.

'Why are you looking at me like that?' Ava asked, tipping her head to one side, her cheeks flushed from alcohol and laughter.

'I'm just wondering what happened to you? You've changed so much since I last saw you. You seem surprisingly level headed. You and your sister used to be quite . . . what's the word? Quite temperamental . . .'

As they drank more and became increasingly familiar, Ava became prettier, more attractive to him. The teenager she'd once been was becoming more apparent in her face.

'Temperamental . . . that's very diplomatic of you.' She swirled the alcohol around her glass.

'Does your sister still live around here?'

'Imogen. No. She died.'

'Shit . . . What happened? I didn't know . . .' Sebastian shifted uncomfortably in his seat, resting briefly on the thought of losing Cecelia.

'She killed herself.'

'Fuck. That's awful. I'm sorry.'

'No you're not.' Ava smiled at him; a reaction that he thought was slightly strange.

Sebastian shrugged. An awkward silence ensued. He wanted to ask her more about it, twin to twin, wondering what it was like to suffer your twin killing herself. It seemed too unbearable to think about. It was something he'd never even considered.

'That's always a conversation killer.' Ava drained the rest of her drink.

'Another?' Sebastian pointed to her glass.

'OK.'

They talked more easily after he returned with another set of drinks. There had been something attractive, endearing almost, about finding out she was now one when she'd been two, as if they had something in common. His separation from Cecelia had been painful and he wondered if it would have been easier if she had been dead. Wanting her, but knowing she didn't want him, seemed worse than not having the choice.

'Have you seen much of Cecelia since you were released?'

'Not really. I don't think she's too keen on the idea. She hasn't visited me, put it that way.'

'Maybe she's waiting for you to come to her. It must be difficult after everything that happened . . .'

'You seem to know a lot about it.' Sebastian's tone was sarcastic but it went unnoticed.

'No, I just read about it in the papers. Only you two know what happened that night at the farm. I'm just talking from the point of view of being a twin. Don't let it destroy your relationship . . . that's all I'm saying.'

Sebastian smiled at her, an image of her naked body being slammed up against his bedroom wall flooded his vision. Standing up, he took her hand and led her out of the pub.

6

Cecelia turned the sign on the shop door round to closed, poured herself a coffee from the percolator that she provided for her customers, and sat down at her large desk which doubled as a counter. She always spent time after she'd closed up tidying the shop and getting everything ready for the next day.

The old Georgian shop had a beautiful atmosphere when it was dark and quiet. Not that it was ever noisy in there – the customers were usually serene and calm – and it was more like visiting a library than a busy shop. She offered three floors of reasonably priced second-hand books and free coffee. After five years of trading it was beginning to become quite a lucrative business.

People rushed past the large window, desperate to get home and out of the rain that had begun to pelt the pavements; April was for once living up to its reputation. She turned her attentions to tidying her desk, switching everything off before she made her way up the two flights of narrow stairs to the attic to check there weren't any customers lurking, lost in their books or asleep in the armchairs, as had happened many times before.

Wandering through the many rooms she picked up discarded books, tidying the shelves as she went. She tried not to think about last week, when Sebastian had stood outside her home – she didn't want her mind to rest on it while she was in the old shop by herself. She felt on edge and it made her look behind her as she moved from room to room. Having reached the top floor, she sat down in one of the tatty old armchairs so she could catch her breath and calm down. Her heart had started to race slightly and she knew it was the turbulence of her mind causing it, the tug of her heart, a yearning she wished would go away. She neatly arranged the books on the table and, now sufficiently calm, she stood up and had one last look around. Her vision took in the window and something outside amongst the threads of people caught her eye. It was as though a strand had come loose from the crowds. She stepped closer to the window and peered through the downpour. There was a narrow alleyway opposite, leading to a Bring and Buy clothes shop. And just shy of the shadow of the path there stood a very young child. As her eyes focused on the figure she realised she looked just like her daughter when she'd been that age. The little girl was staring up at her window and no one else seemed to be aware of her presence.

Cecelia put her hand against the window, feeling the cold pane returning her warmth with steam. To her surprise the child's hand moved up in response, as though in greeting. She turned to look behind her, as if the girl might be waving to someone else, but of course there was no one there. When she turned back to the window the child had gone. Her eyes searched the people passing up and down the road, but she was nowhere to be seen. The shop door slammed below startling her even more; heart pounding she ran down the stairs to tell whoever had come in that the shop was closed.

'Hello!' she called before she'd reached the last set of stairs. 'I'm afraid we're closed.'

There was no answer and Cecelia began to feel slightly unnerved, cursing herself for yet again not locking the front door.

On the shop floor there was no one visible and she reasoned with herself that maybe someone had opened the door, seen the darkness and realised she was closed so had exited again.

She quickly began to grab her things so she could lock up and go home. As she collected the takings and began putting them into her cash tin she saw movement in the shadow of the shelves. She looked up slowly, nausea beginning to rise in her stomach.

'Hello, Cecelia.'

Cecelia's hand flew to her pounding chest.

'What the hell are you doing here?'

'This is quite good.' Sebastian tilted the small hardback book he was holding.

'You shouldn't be here.'

'Shouldn't I?' Sebastian looked up from the shelves and stared right at her.

'No, you shouldn't. I don't really want to see you.' They stared at one another.

'Well, either you do or you don't. I don't *really* want to see you, implies that you're thinking about it.'

Sebastian turned to put the book back where he'd found it and as she watched him the familiarity of his movements began pricking at her skin.

'I don't want to see you like this . . . you can't just turn up with no warning . . . And stop coming to the house, it's making things difficult for me . . .' As soon as the words had left her mouth she wished she could take them back as she felt the letters tumble down her sweater. She didn't want Sebastian to think there was something wrong at home.

Sebastian turned to face her, hands in his pockets. 'Well, since you haven't come to see me since I was released and, knowing you like I do –'

Cecelia raised her hand, feeling a sudden surge of confidence. 'I'm going to stop you there, Sebastian. You don't know me at all –'

He in turn cut her off, raising his finger as if to point at her.

'I know you better than anyone. Remember?' He tipped his head slightly, observing her. 'I decided to come and find you, to show that there are no hard feelings. I understand how guilt can hold a person back. I spent a lot of time thinking about why you wouldn't come and visit me in prison and I get it, I really do.'

Cecelia laughed, more from nerves than anything else. She didn't really know how to respond to what he'd said.

'Come for a coffee with me, Cecelia.' He smiled at her.

She sighed. 'I can't right now. Maybe another day . . .'

'Saturday? You choose where since you know the town better than I do.' The words were carved into a sharp edge. It didn't go unnoticed but Cecelia chose to ignore the pointed inflection.

'OK . . . but just one meeting, that's all . . . I'll meet you in the café across the road. I think you already know it.' She looked at him pointedly.

Sebastian nodded. 'See you there at eleven.'

He moved forwards, arms outstretched to embrace her, and like a see-saw she tipped the opposite way. Awkwardly, he grabbed her arms as if she was about to fall. Firmly, he pulled her forwards and lightly kissed her cheek, hovering briefly, making all the muscles in her body tighten as she felt his breath brush her ear.

When he eventually let go, she stepped backwards. The pull, the thread of what they had once been was still there, ever present, as though it had just been rewired.

He turned in the doorway on his way out.

'You know, you shouldn't leave this door unlocked when you go upstairs. Anyone could walk in.' He grinned, causing the tiny hairs on her forearms to rise, her skin prickling.

'It's good to see you, Mouse.'

7

Sebastian had recognised Caroline as soon as he saw her in the bookshop; he'd spent quite a bit of time watching her from the café across the road, a perfect observatory with its big glass windows and dark interior. Caroline had long, dark red hair and her face was smattered with freckles, highlighting her baby pink coloured lips. Her green eyes were as bright as Cecelia's were dark blue and there was a perfect symmetry about her face that mesmerised him. Her bottom lip had a deep crease in the middle, her almond-shaped eyes set in perfect line with one another.

The day had arrived when Cecelia and Sebastian were due to meet in town, but Sebastian decided that he'd visit Caroline first. He was eager to meet her, regardless of Cecelia's wishes.

Finding out that Cecelia owned a bookshop had given him some glimmer of hope, a way he could reach her without going to the house. The information was vague, the shop being the only outwardly public fact about her life she couldn't hide.

Sebastian stood outside the shop for quite some time, observing the building, the sign and the windows. This was something he hadn't been able to do from his position across the road as the light reflecting on the glass obscured his view. The girl within stared at him, obviously intrigued rather than worried. He realised how familiar he must look to her – the male version of her mother. He smiled and moved towards the door.

'You're my mother's brother, aren't you?' she said, as soon as he entered the shop.

'Yes, and you're Caroline.'

'I am . . . how did you know that?'

Sebastian hesitated; there was a glimpse of someone else in her face, another type of familiarity he wasn't quite sure of. Then it came to him, all the way from eighteen years ago.

'Does my mum know you're here?' There was a wary note in her voice, suggesting to Sebastian that she must know that he and Cecelia didn't get along.

'Yes. I'm just about to meet her for coffee. Didn't she tell you?'

'Errr, no she didn't mention it actually. I've seen you watching me from across the street . . . and outside the school.'

He raised his hand to stop her talking. 'I'm not here to cause trouble; I just want to see my family.'

She nodded. 'I knew there was something going on. She's been acting weird lately . . . well, weirder than normal.' She laughed and then reverted back to her hostility. 'We saw you standing at the gate . . .'

'You're just as beautiful as I remember your mum being at your age.'

Caroline blushed, her shoulders rising slightly in a shrug – she obviously wanted to let him in but wasn't sure if she was allowed to.

'It would be nice if you and mum could sort out your differences. Eighteen years is a long time to hold a grudge.'

'You're right, it is.'

'Are you just visiting, or are you planning on staying for a while?'

He frowned, trying to work out what Cecelia had told Caroline about him. 'I'm staying for the time being.'

'Oh?' She held his gaze, showing him she was far more forthright than Cecelia.

'I take it you know where I've come from?'

'Yes . . .'

He leant forward on the counter and she held her breath.

'I'm not going to hurt you.' He could see the symmetry of her face even more clearly from this angle – the perfect matching brows and almond-shaped eyes. He reached round to the side of her and picked up the case of the CD that was playing quietly in the background.

'Do you work here every Saturday?'

She swallowed and he stepped away from the desk, giving her space to breathe, allowing her to see that he wasn't the monster she thought he was.

'Most Saturdays, yes, and in the school holidays, too . . . look, I shouldn't –'

He cut her off.

'I don't suppose they'll be too many more of those left; you must be nearing exams.'

'Yes . . . I'm in my last year.'

'Radiohead.' He nodded. 'One of my favourites.'

'Are they? I love them.'

He nodded again.

They chatted for a while, Sebastian searching for more common ground. It turned out that Caroline was studying art as he had done in prison.

'I'd better go. It was nice to meet you, Caroline.' He used few words, but he cleverly dripped them along the counter to make her feel guilty for brushing him off. He hadn't been the image of the person she'd painted in her head and, presented with an intelligent, well-dressed man, he knew he had confused her, especially as Cecelia had hidden her meeting with him from her family.

'Nice to meet you, too . . . will we see you again?'

Sebastian opened the door of the bookshop and as the bell tinkled he cast the hook of words she would bite onto.

'Yes, if you want to.'

8

Each minute that passed by saw Cecelia changing her mind about whether to meet Sebastian later that morning or not. She was still in her pyjamas and was staying occupied by cleaning the house from top to bottom, an activity she was obsessed with. Samuel's funeral business was situated not far from the house and it always made her feel unclean – the thought of him washing bodies made her shudder. Disinfecting everything regularly settled her anxiety and the anger that always seemed to be brewing near to the surface. When had their marriage changed? How had they shifted in their relationship from feeling confident and forthright, to anxious and unworthy? She often pondered this, tried to be more assertive, show some confidence. It never lasted; her mental state was always the main consideration. She couldn't be upset or cross or annoyed without it being perceived as a symptom, so little was said in response. This irrationality will pass, was always clear across Samuel's face. So they never really had a discussion about anything, her opinions couldn't be true because her emotional state was out of balance. She wanted to scream, she couldn't get out, felt trapped within the confines of herself and, beyond that, if she ever managed to claw her way to the surface, the solid walls Samuel had created to keep her safe. Even her involuntary muteness, which didn't occur very often now, made her feel suffocated, caused her to panic.

They'd had a bad night, the pair of them. Probably brought on by Cecelia's impending meeting with Sebastian, not that she'd told Samuel where she was going. He liked to keep tabs on her movements. I don't care what you do or where you go, he would so often say, just tell me where you are. But she couldn't tell him about this. There was an underlying jealousy over Sebastian. The tone of his voice changed if she ever mentioned him and he asked a lot of questions she'd answered before. She'd seen it in him before Sebastian went to prison. He was envious of their closeness, their understanding, their symmetry.

Too much bleach on the cloth she was using had begun to burn her hands. She never wore gloves as she liked the smell of the detergents on her skin when she'd finished as proof that she'd cleaned. She was finding it increasingly difficult to decipher reality from dreams. She scratched at her pale and cracked sore hands, which reminded her of the fragile state her mind was in. The sleep-deprived night had put everything out of kilter; the entire day wouldn't slot into its rightful place until it magically altered during the small hours.

Cecelia had seen a ghost. It was something she was certain of. She could see now, though, that announcing this at dinner probably hadn't been the best move. Caroline had kept her head down and stared at the food on her plate as she so often did when she felt uncomfortable, whilst Samuel had calmly told her it must have just been someone amongst the crowd. But she'd seen the child again, several times since she had appeared across the road from the bookshop, and she wasn't mad enough not to know what was real and what wasn't.

Their reaction had caused some indignation, old familiar feelings rising immediately to the surface, making her voice reach a higher pitch than usual. Why couldn't she stay calm, stand firmly by her convictions without getting upset or irate. She felt like an outsider in her own home. This was like the green suitcase on the purlin again. The green suitcase that she remembered so well. The green suitcase that had caused her to leave her bed in the small hours of the night in search of it. She needed to find out what was inside – she knew that it was somehow linked to Yvonne. This was something that happened quite regularly, although Cecelia didn't always remember it. Sometimes she would wake up with leaves and mud stuck to the bottoms of her feet with no memory of how they had got there. There was an element to this sleepwalking that gave her a sense of freedom, of balanced control, knowing her mind could steer her body to go somewhere she didn't know anything about. Occasionally she would wake up in the garden or down the track that led to their house, sometimes she would find herself in the cellar. Cecelia knew she was always in search of the suitcase and on the edge of remembering each time she surfaced. The need to know what was in the suitcase had dispersed briefly when her mother had appeared all those years ago, but the urge had quickly returned. It was important to her, even though she didn't know why.

Last night was different though because she knew she hadn't been asleep this time and she hadn't been looking for the suitcase.

The little girl had started appearing by the side of her bed many years ago. She would always whisper a few words in the cold sharp darkness and lead her by the hand. They would get halfway down the stairs when Samuel would switch the light on and frighten her away. Cecelia hated him for that.

9

The café was fairly full when Sebastian arrived. There was a slightly embarrassing moment when he realised that Cecelia was already sitting down across the room from where he had sat, searching for him as he was for her. Then a few awkward moments as they sorted out some tea and coffee.

'So, we might as well start from the beginning. What's been happening since I've been away? Give me a quick run-down of your life.' Sebastian stirred his coffee as he tried to make Cecelia look at him.

'I'd really rather you didn't talk to Caroline unless I'm with her.'

Sebastian leaned back in his chair and frowned, slightly confused by her hostility towards him. An image from almost two decades ago entered his head of Roger lying on the stairs, Cecelia, semi-naked, holding a gun in her hands.

'Hello, I'm Sebastian, your twin brother.' He awkwardly half raised himself from his seat and held out his hand for Cecelia to shake.

'Don't be an idiot, Sebastian.' She shook her head and stared down at the table.

'Sorry, I just thought you had mistaken me for someone else.' Sebastian turned to look behind him. 'Because, you do remember I was in prison for many years?'

Cecelia shifted uncomfortably in her seat, unable to look at him for more than a few seconds.

'I'm not good at all this ... all this ...' she gestured with her hands. 'Meeting up with people from the past. I'm not the person I used to be ... you don't know me anymore ... you're expecting me to be the same person I was then, but I'm not.'

'Wow, so many clichés in one sentence ... I know you're not the same, Cece, how could you be after all these years? But did you ever think that maybe I'm not the same person either?'

'I know ... but I can't feel something that isn't there ...' Cecelia looked at him properly for the first time. 'I'm sorry ...'

Sebastian leant forward on the table, squeezing his hands in his lap, as if he'd been physically winded. Sighing heavily, he sat up and pulled his dark blond hair through his fingers.

'Listen, Sebastian –'

'Do you want to go and watch a film?' He interrupted her, not wanting her words to do any more damage. 'At the cinema, where we used to go ... I saw it was still open.'

Cecelia frowned. He could see she was unsure where the question had come from. They were completely out of sync with one another, he realised. There had been a time when they'd have thought of the idea together. That's what he was trying desperately to do – re-align their relationship.

'No, Sebastian. I'm not going to the cinema with you, I'm not going anywhere with you.' She was already lifting her bag onto her lap, getting ready to leave.

'Please don't do this, Cece.'

'I'm not doing anything, Sebastian. I just want you to let me get on with my life, for you to get on with yours.' She was looking right at him, stony faced, her entire demeanour completely altered. It was as though a stranger was sitting across from him. 'We've led different lives; we've been apart now for longer than we were together.'

Sebastian watched her face drain of any emotion she might have had for him when they first sat down in the café.

'I'm glad you've managed to convince yourself that you did nothing wrong. It must fit in very nicely with your perfect life. I served eighteen years for you.' Sebastian's words skidded across the table, landing straight in Cecelia's lap. He could almost feel the sharp edges cutting her hands.

'Eighteen years? Oh come on Sebastian! Your sentence was extended because of your bloody temper; you'd have been released a lot earlier if it wasn't for that. So don't try to make out you served all those years because of me. You should be grateful.'

'You make it sound like I owed you!' said Sebastian.

'That's because you did.' The beautiful face he had thought about non-stop for all those years had altered almost beyond recognition as she hissed at him across the table. 'If I hadn't stopped Roger that night, he'd have killed you. Maybe not right then but eventually.'

'Perhaps you should have let him.'

'You're being ridiculous, Sebastian. We're quits; let's just leave it at that.'

Sebastian sat back in his chair as Cecelia picked up her bag ready to leave. A few people had turned to look at the sound of raised voices.

'I need you, Cece.' He realised that returning her spite wasn't going to keep her there and he was desperate to make her stay.

'No you don't, you're just obsessed with someone who doesn't exist anymore.' She laid some money on the table and began pulling her coat on.

Sebastian waited for Cecelia to close the café door and then he followed her, quickly falling in step alongside her. She tried to ignore him, staring straight ahead, but he kept up with her the entire time until she eventually stopped walking and turned in the opposite direction.

'I don't owe you an explanation, Sebastian. Leave me alone.'

As she walked away, Sebastian grabbed her arm hard and pulled her sharply against him.

'Nothing is that simple, Cece.' He spat the words in her ear, making sure they were tucked deep inside her head before he let go of her so abruptly that she stumbled into the gutter.

10

Cecelia froze when she saw Sebastian coming through the shop door; she felt as though her body had been suddenly halted after travelling at high speed and she was waiting for her vital organs to settle, to begin working again. It had been a month or more since she'd seen him at the café. Every day thereafter, she'd felt quite unsettled, worried that he might appear at the shop or, worse still, come to her house again. It hadn't been difficult for him to find out where she lived as they had never left Samuel's childhood home, the foster home where she and Sebastian had lived after Roger died.

A tiny part of her had wanted to see him again. Memories of how they'd once been with one another had filled her mind ever since their meeting and the familiarity of him was drawing her to him. There was something about the safety of someone knowing her as well as he did, even though she'd tried to convince him she'd changed. She'd expected to feel that familiarity with Samuel one day. All those years ago, when they'd first got together, she had thought the feelings would develop as time went on, but she had never felt the same way about him as she did her brother. She had a confusion of emotions for Samuel that she could never decipher or understand. The only reason she'd been aware of it was because she watched Samuel express those emotions about her, telling her things Sebastian once had. It had left her feeling displaced, upside down almost, about why she should have feelings like that towards her brother and he for her. Over the years she consoled herself with the explanation that they were twins and all twins felt that way about one another. Being separated for eighteen years had hardened her resolve; his absence hadn't made her heart grow fonder, it had squeezed it almost to death and that's how it must stay.

'Sorry, what did you say?' asked Cecelia, snapping out of her thoughts.

'Mum has been taken to hospital; she's had a heart attack.'

Cecelia and Sebastian stared at one another.

'A shock, I know. I called through and the nurse I spoke to says she's stable but we need to get over there right away.'

All Cecelia heard was I, I, I. Her attention was slightly distracted by Caroline sitting to her right and Sebastian, whose eyes kept straying to her. They were smiling at one another.

Cecelia turned to look at Caroline, wondering when she and Sebastian had become so familiar with one another. Her daughter's face was flushed pink and she seemed nervous around him. Cecelia looked back at Sebastian and then her daughter again. She'd known he'd been to see Caroline when she was working in the shop and they'd bumped into one another a few times outside school. Caroline had also bombarded Cecelia with lots of questions about him. Questions she hadn't been interested in before she'd met him because she had just seen him as her mum's brother that she didn't have anything to do with. But now Caroline was obviously seeing something different.

Caroline attempted to stand up just as Cecelia put her arm out to gently stop her. It was a small movement magnified by the silence, and, like a fine spray, awkwardness descended.

'Caroline, go and wait for me at home and tell your dad I'm going to be late . . . in fact, don't tell him, I'll call him.'

Caroline nodded and Cecelia noticed that her daughter was unable to look at Sebastian. Cecelia and Caroline knew each other too well, as any parent and child know each other, but Cecelia had always felt like she was looking at another version of herself when she looked at Caroline. And she knew her down to every fibre of her sinew. Cecelia had asked Caroline to meet her at the shop after school because she was becoming suspicious about where she'd been going at the end of each school day. Her daughter had become secretive and had been withdrawing from the family, and Cecelia had an idea why.

Having tried and failed to keep Caroline away from Sebastian, she'd decided to fill her time instead so that she was too busy to see him.

'Go on, off you go.'

Caroline slid off her stool. 'It'll take me ages to walk and it's raining.'

'We could drop her off on the way to the hospital.'

Cecelia glared at Sebastian. 'The hospital's in the opposite direction. No, the fresh air will do her good. Caroline, you've been stuck in a classroom all day. Off you go and I'll see you later. I won't be long.' She looked pointedly at Sebastian.

'Can't I come with you?'

'Home. Now!' Cecelia turned her glare to Caroline, who tutted and left the shop. Cecelia couldn't help feeling like the outsider in this group of three.

Instead of going to pick up her bag, coat and keys, Cecelia walked over to the coffee machine and poured herself a cup and offered one to Sebastian. She didn't feel like rushing to the hospital.

Sebastian took the mug from her hand and placed it on one of the shelves. 'We don't have time for that. Let's go.'

Cecelia reached for the cup and walked slowly back to her seat. She looked at him thoughtfully. 'I don't close for another half an hour. And anyway, I'm not sure I'm going to go to the hospital.'

Sebastian put his hands in his coat pockets to retrieve his cigarette tin. 'I'll go and have this outside. You get sorted, lock up and we'll go.'

Ignoring him, she continued. 'My immediate reaction was to rush over there but then I thought, why would I do that? Why would I go running to the woman who deserted us when we were children and never apologised?'

'What?'

Cecelia tipped her head to one side; she was becoming exasperated at his fake naivety.

'I asked you to leave us alone, Sebastian, but you seem to have struck up a relationship with my daughter.'

'Explain to me why you have so much hatred towards our mother?' Sebastian reverted back to the previous conversation.

'She did the best for us under the circumstances. What has she got to apologise for?'

Cecelia breathed deeply. 'You're right. How arrogant of me to expect her to apologise for leaving us with our psychotic father. Silly me.'

'Cecelia, are you really so petty as to hold a grudge for all these years? Does it really matter now in light of recent events?'

She wanted to slap him really hard. She saw the knife on the window sill at home glinting in her mind's eye. It was always there on the surface. A deep breath and the anger peered round the corner of her emotions, prodding her with a sharp stick, daring her to release it.

'It matters to me!' She stabbed her chest with her finger, desperately trying to keep a grip on what was happening at that moment, but she could feel herself slipping again.

'Look, Cecelia, Mum is in hospital and she's asked to see us. We should go – whatever you think of her, she's still our mother. One thing I learnt in prison was that holding onto the past doesn't help anyone.'

Her skin tightened in irritation. 'Oh, well done you.' She sipped her coffee, dampening her dry throat. 'We were never a real family. We just happen to be related but we don't think the same or have the same morals as other families do. Like my family does.'

'Whatever she has and hasn't done, she always wanted the best for us and, looking back, she probably protected us from things we never knew about.'

'Oh really? That's all a bit convenient, isn't it? Does it make you feel better, believing that?'

'I'm not arguing with you, Cecelia, just saying how I see it.'

'Well, you would see it like that, wouldn't you? I mean, you've never known a real family, not like I have. When you have children of your own, you'll understand how important it is to be a proper parent, a united team.'

Sebastian lifted his head and stared at her beneath his half-closed lids, another trait that irritated her, displaying how much she'd hurt his feelings.

'Very touching, but I still think you should come with me to see her. How would you feel if she died and you hadn't seen her one last time?' He leant both hands on the wooden counter and stared at the floor, causing his blond hair to flop forward. She could hear a slight noise, as though he was muttering to himself.

'Pardon?'

Sebastian looked up abruptly and tapped both hands on the counter.

'Come on, let's get going'

There was a long silence where they both defiantly stared at one another.

'If I decide to come, that is the end of it. I need you to under-stand that, Sebastian. She is nothing to me.' As she heard her harsh words she felt a jolt deep within her. She couldn't work out in her mind whether she really felt nothing for Yvonne, or if she still hated her. She felt like she was tricking herself; saying one thing, feeling another. She'd received a letter a short while ago – something she wasn't prepared to talk to Sebastian about at this time – telling her that Yvonne had legally transferred the farm to her and Sebastian. This had only made Cecelia even angrier. The farm reminded her too much of Roger and all that had happened there over those years. She was astounded that Yvonne hadn't realised how painful that would be for her. Cecelia wouldn't care if the farmhouse went up in flames; she didn't want anything to do with the past. She'd moved forward and now there were too many hands pulling her back.

Now she had to break the control she felt her mother was trying to drape over her. There had been no clause in Yvonne's letter or the subsequent one from her solicitor, no stipulations as she would have expected. And for her this was all wrapped up with whether or not she should visit Yvonne in hospital. Deep inside, she wanted to visit her, show her what she'd become without any parental support, gloat in some way. But this was all a lie, one she knew her mother would see through.

Sebastian was outside with his back to the window, smoking a cigarette. She quickly rummaged through her bag for her tablets and took one with a swig of her coffee that had turned cold along with her insides. The doctor had told her that they would calm and balance her. Taking a deep breath she flicked the lights, grabbed her things and left, much to the apparent surprise of Sebastian.

Most of the journey was made in silence apart from Sebastian pointing out things that had changed – shops and businesses that had been replaced with new ones – which irritated Cecelia further. She didn't answer him, just left him with his wistful observations. All she wanted to think about was getting parked at the hospital, visiting Yvonne for an acceptable amount of time, dropping Sebastian off and getting back to the sanctuary of her home.

There were all sorts of things trying to push their way into her mind, one of which was her need to talk to Samuel properly about Sebastian, in a calm and considered way, so that he understood why she didn't want anything to do with her twin. As well as a need to explain to Caroline, without giving away too much, why she wasn't allowed to see her uncle. Turning to look at Sebastian as they paused at some traffic lights, she was becoming acutely aware of how much of a threat he was. He wasn't hiding anything, well not that she was aware of, but he knew things about her she'd never told anyone. She needed to keep him separate from her world, and her sanctuary. She didn't want anybody to intrude on that, especially not her brother. The problem was, she was losing control of Caroline and had very little influence over what she was doing. The most important thing for Cecelia right now was that Sebastian didn't find out anything else about their lives – that could only put her in a vulnerable position. Without prompting, Sebastian brought up the conversation himself, as though he were reading her mind.

'What are we going to do with the farm?'

'You received a letter too?'

'Yes, but Mum told me a while ago.' Sebastian pulled his seat belt away from him, turned in his seat and leant his head against the window, facing her side on.

Cecelia's jaw clenched in unison with her hands on the steering wheel. She was now wishing she'd taken more than one tablet. She needed it, dealing with Sebastian. 'I didn't know you'd seen Mum since you got out.'

'I never knew you lived with her.' He seemed to get comfortable in his seat as his eyes burnt into the side of her face. She was now beginning to regret her decision to go to the hospital.

'Briefly . . . it didn't work out.' She wanted to say more but the words tripped and fell from her lips, skidding on her lap, landing under the pedals of her car. She pressed her foot down on the accelerator. She needed to keep her balance.

'How long have you been with Samuel?' Sebastian knew the answer but he wanted to make a point.

'Long enough. Stop looking for something that isn't there.'

'I'm just interested, that's all.'

'When did you see Mum? How do you even know she's in hospital?' Cecelia slowed the car, wondering if he was lying about the whole thing.

'I live with her. In your old rooms actually.'

The noise of the handbrake as she parked the car split the crackling atmosphere between them.

'What?'

'Where did you think I lived?'

Sebastian chuckled to himself, irritating her further. She had to get a grip on this situation. She could feel herself stepping into the other side, the place she had left and didn't want to return to.

'I don't care about any of that; I just want you to stay away from Caroline. She doesn't need you in her life.'

They both stepped out of the car. The rain was beginning to fall harder.

'Caroline is eighteen, I can't stop her doing what she wants to do . . . believing what she wants to believe. She asks a lot of questions . . .'

'She's seventeen, actually, and she'll do what I tell her.'

'What are you going to do, Cece? Call the police?'

'Do you understand what I've said?' The words skidded across the rain-soaked roof of her car splashing at his feet.

'Over and out.' He saluted, angering her, mocking her.

Assuming she was taking the lead and he was following her she made her way up the hill towards the dirty whitewashed building, the rain pelting them both. Instead of going through the main entrance, Cecelia led Sebastian round the back towards the mortuary, a place she knew well, having driven Samuel there to collect bodies on many occasions.

'Where are we going?' Sebastian easily matched Cecelia's forceful, angry strides.

As they reached the back entrance she led him under a covered area normally frequented by smokers.

'I didn't know you smoked, Cecelia.' He grinned at her, firing up her temper further as he reached for his tobacco tin.

With all her physical strength she grabbed his face and rammed his body against the wall.

'Listen to me, you cunt. Keep your mouth shut and stay away from my family. Because if you don't . . .' she banged his head against the wall to emphasise how much she meant what she was saying. '. . . because if you don't . . . I'll kill you.'

She let go of his face, her temper subsiding, adrenalin and her medication flooding her veins, the peak of the vent having been released.

Sebastian didn't move, he just stared at her, and within the depths of his shock at her outburst she could see a look that was all too familiar, a hint of adoration.

Rubbing his cheek where she'd grabbed it, she expected him to say something, at least make a comical reference to the language she'd just used. But he didn't, he just stared, considering her as he rolled a cigarette.

Having said what she needed to and with no apparent retaliation, Cecelia moved away from him, but as she turned Sebastian grabbed her by the arms and rammed her against the adjacent wall, knocking the breath out of her. Her mouth opened as she gasped for breath and he quickly covered it with his own. She struggled, pressing the back of her head into the rough brick wall, desperate to get away from him. She managed to pull her face to one side, breaking their mouths apart, but in doing so causing him to run his tongue across her face. He held her there for a few moments; she could feel his hot breath in her ear, as she began to shake against him. Once he released his grip she hit him repeatedly around his head, his shoulders, anywhere she could as he tried to restrain her arms. Getting the better of her he pushed her against the wall again, trapping her with his forearm across her neck, choking the air from her lungs.

'You will never speak to me like that again,' he seethed at her, leaving more spittle on her face.

As soon as he let go of her she began frantically wiping her face and mouth with the sleeve of her jacket, the brown leather mixing with the taste of his saliva, which was now mixed with her salty tears.

Out of breath she watched him light his cigarette, completely unfazed.

'What you need to remember, Cece, is that I love you. And everything I've ever done has been because of that.'

His ice-encrusted words made the skin across her shoulders and up the back of her neck prickle.

'But the thing is, Sebastian,' she sobbed, 'that I hate you.'

11

The stark, crudely lit hospital corridor seemed to close in on Sebastian as he looked for the room where his mother was being treated. Cecelia had left without visiting Yvonne. He was not in the best of moods but he was satisfied that he'd finally managed to raise so much emotion from his sister.

Eventually finding his mother, Sebastian entered the room and pulled a chair up to the side of her bed and sat down. Yvonne seemed to have aged rapidly since she had been brought into hospital. She looked dehydrated and even her hair seemed to have turned grey overnight. She was also very out of breath. 'You need to quit those fags, Mother.' He reached for her hand.

'Hark, who's talking. Do you know, I don't think I would smoke now even if I could?' Yvonne lifted her head slightly and breathed in. 'You smell of paint.'

'No flies on you, even when you're ill. You know you'll need to take better care of your health when you get out of here?'

'I won't be coming out of here, Sebastian.' Yvonne leant back into her raised pillows.

'Don't talk daft. You're just tired.'

'I need to talk to you about something.'

'Sounds very serious.' Sebastian shifted uncomfortably on his chair.

'I want you to know I don't care what you or Cecelia do with the farm as long as it doesn't involve me.'

'I didn't even know you still owned the farm until you told me . . . why have you kept it for so long?'

'I don't know, son. Memories, I suppose. I didn't feel right getting rid of it too quickly. Thought one of you two might need it, or that you'd want to get the farm working again after you were released. I see now that's not something you would want to do. It's strange, but I just kept thinking Roger would come back and would need somewhere to go, even though I know he's dead. I suppose it was because I wasn't there when he died. Do you understand what I mean?' She gripped his hand tighter. 'But it's time for me to let go.'

'Whatever you want to do, Mum.'

'I don't know what Cecelia's going to say about it. Whether I gave her half or not, I'd be doing the wrong thing.'

'I'll talk to her about it, try not to worry.' Sebastian was pleased he had another excuse to visit Cecelia.

'You've seen her?'

'Of course I have. She's my twin sister.'

Yvonne searched his face, waiting for him to tell her more, expand on what he'd said.

'Do you know, when you were children, I always thought it was you who was the strange child.'

'What made you think that?'

'I don't know, just a feeling I suppose. Have you met Caroline?'

'Yes, I've had coffee with her a couple of times after school.'

'Oh. You never said . . .'

Sebastian realised he was making his relationship with Cecelia and Caroline sound better than it actually was, but he didn't want Yvonne to think there was a problem. And he wasn't really lying – he had spent some time with Caroline after school, it was just that Cecelia didn't know about it.

'She's a stunning girl – very confident, grownup for her age. A more defined version of Cecelia, I think.'

'I wouldn't know; it's been quite a few years since I've seen her properly. I always thought she was more forthright than her sister.' Yvonne's voice was becoming distant, weak.

Sebastian frowned, unsure of what he'd heard. The words repeated in his head. 'Sister? Cecelia has more children?'

'Had. Caroline was a twin. Lydia died when they were nine. She was involved in an accident outside the school. I'm surprised Cecelia didn't mention it when you saw her.'

'I'm surprised you didn't mention it when you visited me in prison.' Sebastian was trying to absorb the information that Caroline, like him and Cecelia, had been part of a pair.

'There's a lot I didn't tell you when you were in prison. I didn't want to upset you.'

'That's quite a big piece of news to keep from me. To not know my sister gave birth to twins and then one of them died.' He ran the name Lydia through his head, counting the letters, trying out the name. 'What happened to her?'

'It was an accident,' Yvonne said again.

'I know, you said. What sort of accident?'

'She was hit by a car outside the school. Died on the way to hospital.'

'Oh. That must have been really hard for Caroline to cope with . . . Cecelia too.'

'Yes, it was hard for everyone. Cecelia hasn't ever come to terms with it, I don't think. Blamed herself, you know? Maybe she's started to move on now. But then, you can never tell with Cecelia. She's always been a temperamental creature.' Yvonne shifted in the bed, trying to get comfortable.

'What happened between the two of you? It must be pretty bad for you not to have spoken to one another for all these years.'

'It's Cecelia who has the problem with me, not the other way round,' Yvonne snapped.

'It doesn't matter who's got a problem with whom – the point is you don't talk to one another.'

'She's never forgiven me for leaving you two all those years ago – it's as simple as that.'

'There's more to it, surely?'

'No, there really isn't.' Yvonne closed her eyes, shutting herself off from him, not wanting to talk about the past.

Sebastian suddenly stood up and kissed Yvonne's forehead. 'Night, Mum.'

'Night, son,' Yvonne said to him as he reached the door.

Halfway down the corridor Sebastian passed someone he recognised. Both men stopped walking and turned to look at each other.

'What are you doing here?' Sebastian said to a slightly shocked Samuel.

'I'm here to see Yvonne.'

'What for?' Sebastian moved defensively towards him. Samuel was greyer, thinner than he'd remembered from the glimpse of him he'd got in the garden.

Samuel shifted uncomfortably on the spot. 'I just need to talk to her about something.'

'Yvonne's asleep. Let's go down to the café, there's something I'd like to talk to you about.'

12

It was the first time in quite a few years that Cecelia had visited the farmhouse, the place she'd spent the first fifteen years of her life. Fifteen years under Roger's rule with a pathetic Yvonne floating in the background. She thought of her now, weak and sickly in her hospital bed. It was beyond Cecelia why she was hanging on to her life so fiercely when she'd spent so much of it so unhappy. Then she thought of her own relationship with Samuel and realised she was possibly doing a similar thing under a different set of circumstances. Another fraction of information that she stored in the various drawers of her mind that she didn't wish to delve through.

Cecelia sighed as she stood outside the old green chipped front door of the farmhouse. She looked around at the garden, which, despite being full of buds, had always felt bleak, even in the summer.

The house was still the same – she didn't know why this surprised her since there was no one living there to alter it. The patchwork fields loomed in the distance. She was always shocked by the stark flatness of the Fenlands and much preferred living across the border in Norfolk where even in the midst of winter it felt cheery and welcoming. Alive, somehow, compared to the flat energy she always felt when she visited the old farmhouse. It felt more like that today. There was a finality about the atmosphere as she unlocked and opened the door with her old set of keys.

Shivering, she went in and quickly moved the old heavy curtain that hung behind the door. It snagged as she'd opened it, giving her a momentary trapped feeling. Once she was on the other side of the curtain, she stood with her back to the large hall. On seeing the staircase, the memory of her father was all too clear – that brief moment of shock on his face, the blankness in his eyes that had slowly eclipsed any sign of life.

She reached out and tried the light switch, turning it on and off a couple of times. She had not expected it to work but to her surprise it did. She wondered why her mother had continued to pay for the electricity when she hadn't lived in the house for quite some years.

The light was dim even though the bulb hung far below the grubby shade. It reminded her of a photographer's developing room. The wind pushed the door closed behind her and her heart was pounding in time with the rattling window panes. There was a strange smell in the air – of long ago gravy dinners, cigarettes and embers from logs burnt away.

Cecelia opened the door to her left and walked into the sitting room. It was just as it had been when she was a child. There were two tatty mustard-coloured sofas which had always reminded her of the Viennese biscuits her mother used to make when she was a child. There were also two dark green velour armchairs at the end of the room situated by the large bay window.

The patterned carpet swirled in front of her, making her feel slightly dizzy. She stepped further into the room and noticed that the seventies wall lights and Anaglypta paper were dusty with dirt, as though they had been sprinkled with black pepper.

The sun began to peek through the grey clouds and was filling the room with light. Cecelia walked over to the window and looked out across the patchwork blanket of fields.

Her phone began to ring, startling her in the shadowy chill of the house. It was Samuel, wondering where she was. It was half-day closing at the bookshop on a Wednesday and she knew he'd be expecting her home early, suffocating her with his concern.

She lied and told him she was rearranging the shop and that she'd pick up some dinner on the way home. Their conversation was strained, stilted, as communication had been between them for some time. They were just two human beings sharing some sort of life together, but he was more interested in her than she was in him. She always seemed to have her back turned towards him.

As she put her phone in her coat pocket she looked back out of the window, her eye catching movement just beyond the garden and across the first patch of fields. A figure was standing on the edge of the closest ditch. She moved nearer to the window, squinting to try and get a better view. It was a woman, she could make out that much. Cecelia thought she looked like Yvonne, but she knew that wasn't possible. She ran out of the sitting room and up the stairs – all memories of Roger now vanished – and down the long corridor leading to the bedroom directly above so she could get a better view from the window there. The figure hadn't moved and Cecelia was even more convinced that the woman looked like her mother. How she remembered her from old photos, rather than how she looked these days. Her shoulder length brown curls were blowing in the bitter wind and she was wearing an outfit that Cecelia remembered very well, a royal blue turtleneck and a tweed skirt. Cecelia was transfixed by the figure, frightened to turn away in case she vanished. She could have sworn she was looking back up at her through the window from the field below. She ran back to the corridor and then into each room that gave a view of that particular part of the fields. The woman appeared in every window pane, just standing and staring at the house.

Cecelia lifted her hand to touch the cold glass and the figure outside raised hers tentatively, as though in response to a wave. Cecelia's fingers slipped down the window. It was her mother, she just knew it, but that wasn't possible – Yvonne was in hospital. She put her finger up to signal for the woman to wait where she was and left the room. She ran downstairs and out the front door and continued around the back of the house, stopping abruptly when she reached the grass. She frantically looked up at the windows and then back in the direction of the fields, but the figure had gone. Cecelia turned on the spot, looking around her in case the woman had moved towards the house, but she knew that was ridiculous. The fields were bleak and sparse and the ditches were far too deep for anyone to get across in a hurry. Maybe she'd been seeing things.

Cecelia wrapped her arms around herself to shut out the cold and tried to rub some comfort into her limbs. It had been a difficult few weeks one way and another and her sleepwalking episodes were beginning to merge with her reality, making her feel unsure of true events. Grey clouds passed across the sun, making it overcast until the sun's rays burst through the perforations. Tepid raindrops landed on her face and she shivered as she smelt the all too familiar steely freshness of the rain that had depressed her so much as a child.

Wandering back into the house she began to feel strangely uneasy. She went upstairs to look out of the windows to see if the figure was there now that she was back inside. It was as though the panes of glass might be carrying a moving picture of the past. In her mind everything in the house was exactly how it had always been except it all looked much older, more tired and shabby.

Walking into the last bedroom she'd been in, she stared out of the window. She scanned the fields but they were empty and still, apart from a gentle shower that was beginning to trickle down the windows, distorting her view. She became aware of her handprint on the window and traced it with her finger. That was when she noticed the much smaller handprint next to hers. Steam from the outline was still visible on the pane. She turned to look around the room, suddenly unnerved. She took in the dusty floorboards, the faded yellow floral duvet which lay across a chipped iron bedstead with no mattress. Apart from an old squat 1940s wardrobe in the corner, the room was empty and echoic.

She turned back to the window again and gasped loudly as the sight of her own reflection in the window startled her.

Her feet suddenly felt like lead weights and she stayed still as she allowed her heart to calm. She frowned at the tiny handprint, quite faded now, but still visible next to hers on the window. The carcass of a large moth lay on the sill along with various flies, reminding her of death and his cloaked darkness.

Out of the corner of her eye Cecelia was sure she'd glimpsed movement across the fields again, although it was becoming harder to see with the gentle rain, and leaning forward she peered through the window. As her eyes focused on the glass of the window she became aware of the reflection of another face just behind hers. She let out a scream as she spun around and saw the bedroom door slam.

Her feet stuck to the spot, her skin prickled and her heart felt as though it was gripping the bars of her ribcage. Pressing her hand to her chest she took some deep breaths, trying to calm herself and quell the sickness rising in her throat. She felt trapped and wanted to get out of the house, but didn't dare move from the room. The light was beginning to fade and she wanted more than anything to be back in the safety of her own home.

After a few moments she decided to brave the bedroom door. She convinced herself that she was tired and more overwrought than she'd realised, and explained away the slamming door as being caused by a draught.

Tentatively she opened the door, her hands shaking. She stepped into the corridor feeling as though her legs didn't belong to her body. Looking both ways down the empty corridor she made a run for it and pelted down the stairs, straight out of the front door. She looked behind her the whole time as she fumbled with the lock.

Getting into the car, she flicked the central locking immediately, telling herself again she was being ridiculous. She turned the key in the ignition and sat for several moments waiting for the car to heat up. She'd gone to the house in search of answers. The green suitcase still haunted her dreams but she had struggled to stay in the gloomy farmhouse long enough to search for it. The last few years had been filled with other traumas, making it difficult for her to concentrate on the past for any length of time.

Staring up at the large building, she remembered the now blurred stories from when she was a child, the fear still painfully real. Her understanding of what had happened was far more prominent now she was an adult and had a child of her own.

As she scanned the house she realised she'd left the hall light on – she could see it glowing brightly through the tiny window above the front door as the darkness from outside became deeper. She turned the car ignition off, preparing herself to quickly go back into the house and flick the switch. She couldn't risk a house fire, whatever her feelings about the place, but everything was telling her not to go back in. She felt sick with the dilemma.

Unclicking her seatbelt, she pulled the handle on the door, releasing the central locking. She paused before opening the car door defiantly. She stopped as her foot touched the gravel and she saw the light in the window disappear, as though someone had gently extinguished the glow from the entire house with a large blanket. She pulled her leg back into the car, slammed the door and locked it once again. Turning the key in the ignition she drove away, telling herself the rain must have caused a power cut. She checked her rear-view mirror, watching the house curve away from her as if it was moving scenery. She slammed on the brakes too late as her car ploughed into a little girl standing on the driveway.

13

Ava turned out to be a good subject for Sebastian's artwork. He now found the faults in her frame to be interesting. He could be rough with her – contort her into all sorts of positions, even hurt her at times – but she seemed to like it, as he tried to adjust her skeletal form, pressing his thumb along the ridges of her bones, feeling them beneath her skin as he moulded her into positions for him to draw.

'Put the cotton wool up your nose, I'm just about ready.' Sebastian was on the floor measuring and cutting pieces of linen for his work.

'Won't the powder fall into my eyes and mouth?' Ava was completely naked and lying on a decorator's sheet on the floor.

'Keep them shut. I want to print the natural line of your features. I'm trying out some new colours instead of my usual black.'

'You're very serious when you're working aren't you?' Ava stood up and began to wander around his room, looking at the pictures, the linen pieces he'd already produced.

'The shoulder blades didn't really work did they? I think you should stick to hands and faces, they're such an interesting subject, don't you think?'

Sebastian didn't answer her; he rarely spoke when he was concentrating. He liked spending time with Ava – she was good company in the main, and she enjoyed posing for him while he sat in the bath, although she usually ended up in there with him.

That said, Ava wasn't Cecelia and she never would be. They were similar in hairstyle and eye shape, but Ava was much taller and willowy, despite her lopsided body. There had always been a slight inhibition to Cecelia; even though she never had a problem wandering around half-naked when they were at the farm, there had been a shyness Sebastian had found endearing. It was always apparent when he was focusing on her from an artist's perspective.

Ava was all too ready to pose and never volunteered to sit naturally. For the first five minutes of their sessions she acted as though she'd turned up to a modelling shoot. It always took him a while to settle her down, stop her pouting, get her to close her legs and reveal a little less, but once she relaxed he enjoyed the company. That was as long as it was on his terms and she didn't just turn up unannounced. This could put him in a bad mood for the rest of the evening as he was still used to a structured timetable.

'You don't talk about your sister much,' Sebastian said when they were both sat in the bath together later that night.

'Neither do you.' Ava sipped her wine and placed it on the bath rack Sebastian used to lean his sketch book on.

'There's nothing to say about her, that's why.'

'I can see how much you love her, regardless of any hostility.'

'I never said I didn't. It goes without saying; she'll always be my Cecelia.'

'When Imogen and I were younger, we thought it was weird that you were twins.'

'What do you mean?' Sebastian poured some more wine from the bottle.

'It sounds funny saying it now but it was because you were a girl and a boy. We didn't know different gender twins existed. Silly, isn't it?'

Sebastian watched droplets of water run down her warm skin to the top of her breasts floating in the milky water.

'I can see why you'd think that.' He laughed. 'We were fascinated at how you could be mirror twins. Especially Cece. She started telling people we were mirror twins too.'

This made them both laugh. 'She was a sweet little girl. I remember when Imogen and I frightened her in that old war bunker. We never saw her again after that . . .'

'I never thought we'd be apart, you know . . .' Sebastian was staring absently into the water, seeing Cecelia laughing as he chased her along the corridors at the farmhouse. Then he saw her standing in the hall, the .22 rifle by her side.

Ava pulled her arms forward as though she was going to embrace herself. 'I do know, yes.'

'Why did your sister kill herself?'

Reaching forward for her glass, Ava gulped her wine, refilling it immediately.

'Lots of reasons really. I suppose you never know what finally tips someone over the edge. We'd been in a few foster homes;

most of the people who ran them were nice, kind. As kind as someone could be when they had unruly adolescent strangers in the house. Then we were separated because there wasn't room anywhere for both of us. It was terrible – we hated living apart. Imogen wasn't as lucky as me and went to a place where one of the foster parents abused her. Sexually. She didn't tell me until later when social services found us a place where we could be together.' Ava reached down to the floor and opened another bottle of wine. 'I wanted to kill him when I found out. Really kill him, I mean. The anger was so bad it burned inside me. It was as though I wouldn't be able to breathe if I didn't let it out, you know?'

Sebastian nodded. 'What happened to him? Was he caught?'

'No. The bastard died ... he fell asleep pissed one night, choked on his own vomit.'

'That's one less paedophile to worry about ...'

'Actually, Imogen didn't see it like that. It tortured her more that he'd died, like he was out of her grip and there was nothing she could do about it. She told me afterwards that the only thing that comforted her, helped her to sleep at night, was imagining how she would kill him. Every night she would think of a different way. She lost it after that and I spent years pulling her back onto the raft.'

'Everyone deals with trauma differently.'

'Yes, so now you can see that I know how you felt all those years ago. I know what it feels like to want someone dead.'

Sebastian was silent. He was slightly irritated that she should compare her story to his. 'Did you find her?' he lit a cigarette.

'Who else do you think it would be?' she said as though he was stupid. 'I knew she was going to do it. I came home from work every day with the anticipation of finding her, and every day I felt grateful she was alive, elated if she was smiling. It really teaches you to appreciate every moment.'

Sebastian spluttered slightly on his wine, wiping his mouth with the back of his forearm. 'It was quite recent then? In the house you're in now?'

'Yes. Just three years ago . . . I won't ever sell it. People think it's weird that I've stayed. But she's there with me.'

It was after hearing that last sentence a sudden realisation dawned on Sebastian. 'I can't imagine losing Cece.'

'Yes you can. You just can't bear to think about the pain it would cause you. I had no option but to explore it because it was inevitable.'

'Do you think you'll ever come to terms with it? Such a huge loss.'

Ava took the refilled glass from his hand. 'I don't want to "come to terms with it" as you put it. If I stop grieving for Imogen, I'll lose her altogether.'

Sebastian thought about this long after Ava had gone home. He envied the clean, perfect memory she had of her twin. She was no longer around to tarnish Ava's memories of her. Some people were better off dead.

14

Cecelia slowly stepped out of the car and looked at the child curled up on the track.

'You're not real, you're not real. You are not real . . .' she whispered over and over again as she pulled herself out of the car and around the bonnet as though she was on the edge of a tall building. Crouching down she reached out to touch the small, still body lying in front of her. Everything was familiar about her – clothes, hair, size, age; her daughter, her Lydia.

Cecelia couldn't bring herself to touch her. She closed her eyes for a few moments, expecting the child to have disappeared when she opened them again. But she was still there, lying on her side, eyes blank. Cecelia stood up, walked a few paces and turned around, only to be faced with the same scene.

'Stop it!' she screamed, pulling at her hair, smacking the side of her head with the heel of her hand. 'Stop it! Stop it! Stop it!' She sat down on the gravel track and sobbed into her knees, pulling them tight into her chest as she had when she was a child. Tears subsiding, she looked up only to discover that the figure in the middle of the unmade road that she thought was Lydia was in fact a deer. Wiping the snot from her nose, she pulled herself forward and sat up, gasping deep sobs as she crawled forward and threw herself onto the large dead beast, its body still warm.

'I'm so sorry, I am so, so, sorry,' she whispered into its dirty flank, her heart settling and her body calming. It was just a ghost.

Eventually, Cecelia stood up, brushed the muck off her jeans and wiped her hands with a tissue she'd found up her sleeve. Using what little strength she had left, she pulled the creature as best she could to the side of the track, onto the grass verge.

Still shaking, she got back into the car and drove to the hospital to see Yvonne. For the first time in many years she realised she needed her mother. It had been many years since she'd last seen her, apart from the odd glimpse in the town. Yvonne was part of a horrible time in her life and, as she'd wanted to do with Sebastian, she'd separated herself from memories of her past life. But now there were things she wanted to talk to her about, the green suitcase being one.

The person she discovered in the hospital bed was familiar to her, but the connection that she was her mother seemed to have slipped away.

Shock turned to apprehension and then a slight smile on her mother's face as she realised who it was.

'I'm pleased you've finally come.' She pushed herself up in the bed. She was weak but there was still harshness in her tone.

'What have the doctors said?' Cecelia patted down her blond hair, still dishevelled from earlier.

Yvonne ignored her question. 'Where's Caroline, I haven't seen her in so long?'

'I'll bring her another time.'

'Has she left school? She must be at college by now.' Yvonne coughed, her chest rattling.

'Sixth form. She's just started her second year.'

Yvonne nodded. 'Are you all right? You look a bit . . . well, a bit of a mess to be honest.'

'I'm fine. I hit a deer in the road. Shook me up a bit, that's all.'

'Did you give it first aid?' Yvonne nodded towards Cecelia's jacket, to the blood stains patterning the left side.

'I'm not here to talk about a fucking deer, Mother.' She snapped, startling Yvonne somewhat. 'Sorry, but I'm not in the mood for jokes.'

'OK, what are you here for then?'

'I just need to ask you something.'

'I know what you've come for, you want to know why I signed half the farm over to you despite the fact you killed your father.'

Cecelia flinched at the words, as they hit her like shards of glass. She walked over to the window so she could think about what to say next.

'If you knew that, why did you sign half the farm over to me? Why not give it all to Sebastian.'

'I didn't know for sure. You just told me.'

They were briefly interrupted by someone with a tea trolley and irritatingly for Cecelia, Yvonne chatted to the waitress as she poured her a hot drink. She sat down in the plastic chair in the corner of the room, arms folded, protecting herself until the woman had left.

'So, now you've given me something you don't think I deserve, you can have it back.'

'I'd have still signed it over. I like the feeling I've given you something we both know you don't deserve. You keep it, or sell your half to your brother.'

'Nice.' Cecelia got up to leave.

'Before you walk out all indignantly, what was it you came here to ask me?'

'I didn't even come here to talk about the fucking farm!' Cecelia was crying, tears streaming down her face. She felt like a child again, like she used to around her mother.

'Then sit down and say what you have to say.'

Cecelia didn't sit down, she stood at the bottom of her mother's bed, feeling as though she was a stranger.

'It doesn't matter now. I'll work it out for myself.'

'Come and sit down.' Yvonne patted the space next to her. 'This might be the last time we see each other. Let's not part on bad terms.'

Reluctantly, Cecelia sat down towards the end of the bed. She wanted to let it all go, release the anger she felt towards her parents, but memories flickered in her mind of times when she'd been frightened of Roger, times when her mother left them to defend themselves and then the last time, when they'd thought she was dead.

'Tell me about that green suitcase in the loft.'

Yvonne fell silent. 'What do you want to know about that for?'

'I don't know why but I keep dreaming about it. Ever since I saw it. I just wondered whose it was and why it appeared in the loft after you left?'

'You thought I was dead that day, didn't you?'

'What day? What are you talking about?'

Yvonne tipped her head slightly. 'The day I left the farm . . .'

'Yes . . . I did . . .' Cecelia snatched some tissues from her mother's table and wiped her nose. 'It was an accident, Mum. You and Dad were arguing; I didn't mean to hurt anyone.'

Yvonne took a deep breath. 'The case was your father's. It was filled with photos of his mother, things she gave him before she left.' She sounded terse, abrupt, as though she'd had enough of the conversation.

'I don't understand.'

'I don't expect you to. You've never understood anything outside your own life. Never tried. Your Dad kept the case. We had a deal after we got married and he saw that I struggled with things . . .'

'What things?' Cecelia was becoming increasingly agitated.

'Having you and Sebastian changed me . . . I couldn't cope with it sometimes. You must remember me going away when you were little?'

'Occasionally, yes . . .'

'Your Dad made me promise that if I ever felt like I might do something rash . . . if I felt out of control – that I might hurt myself or one of you – that I would take that green suitcase, pack it with my things and never come back. It would be a code between us that I had reached my limits, that I couldn't cope anymore. His mother left the case behind and he told me he knew, even at that young age, what she'd gone to do. He thought it was better for a mother to leave her children rather than commit suicide.'

'I still don't understand. Is that it?'

'Yes, that's it. His mum killed herself when he was a child and he didn't want you and Sebastian to suffer the same. If I was ever to come downstairs with the green suitcase, he would know that was it, our marriage was over. Whenever I went away without it, he knew I was going to come back.'

'He told us his mother left them all and he never saw her again.'

Yvonne sipped her tea. 'Suicide was really taboo in those days. Most doctors wouldn't even write it on a death certificate.'

'It didn't stop him being an arsehole though, did it?'

'You need to appease your conscience, I understand that.'

'Don't preach that religious bollocks to me.' Cecelia got up from the bed, collecting her car keys from the table. 'You were terrible parents and didn't deserve to have children.'

Yvonne laughed. 'You barely gave your father a chance to show you what a good parent he could be.'

'A good parent? You have to be joking. You're mad!'

'Say what you like, Cece. You've always blamed us for your life, never taken responsibility for your own decisions.'

'That's rich! You'll be telling me next it was my fault Lydia died!'

Yvonne shrugged and stared at her, inflaming Cecelia's already frail temper.

'Do you know what? I wish I'd put that bullet right through your head.' She spat the words out, watching them slide down Yvonne's face.

15

Sebastian moved casually through the throng of teenagers as they chatted, completely distracted by school gossip, their mobiles, and who had what food to offer.

They naturally moved to make way for him, without even noticing his presence.

He paused amidst the jostling to retrieve a cigarette from his jacket pocket and check his phone, wanting it to look like he just happened to be walking that way.

A mixture of young adolescents pushed past him and he swayed in time with their movements. He looked up from lighting his cigarette just as Caroline came into view with her friends. He'd seen her in the distance some minutes before as she'd pushed her way from the entrance to the school along with all the other teenagers desperate to leave the confines of their education.

Stepping off the pavement, wanting to seem casual, he put himself in line with her path. They'd chatted the last few weeks, even gone for coffee. They shared a love of art and he had impressed her with talk of his original techniques. He knew Cecelia had told Caroline about his time in prison to try to convince her to stay away from him, but it hadn't worked. Caroline had seen something different within the picture her mother was painting for her – the numbers weren't matching up with the colours.

Walking more slowly, he allowed the crowds to pass, intent on looking busy with his phone until, stepping back onto the pavement, he was exactly in her eyeline as she approached with her friends. He turned just as she spotted him. A glint of a smile lifted Caroline's lips as recognition lit her face. It was working, he thought to himself. She was warming to him. He had been casually bumping into her since their first meeting and he could see that contrary to what she'd been told, she was making her own mind up about him.

Caroline's friends acknowledged him briefly and moved on with the crowd as Sebastian and Caroline stood on the pavement as everyone passed.

'Going straight home today?'

She hesitated. 'I don't have to … We could go for coffee again?'

Sebastian looked at his phone to give her the impression that he was busy.

'Sorry, I thought you were asking –'

'No, no, it's fine. I was actually going to the café anyway but I've just remembered I need to get home for a delivery.'

'OK.' Caroline shrugged and looked along the school crowds, at her friends up ahead, wanting to catch up with them.

'Tell you what, why don't you come over to mine for a coffee?'

Sebastian knew the answer to this because he'd watched her over the last few weeks and observed that she never went straight home to her parents, instead choosing to go to a café if she wasn't required to work in the bookshop.

'I'm not sure . . .' She shrugged again. 'What would Mum say?'

He leant in towards her, a wry smile across his lips. 'Does she need to know?'

Her hesitation was endearing. She wanted to go with him but needed his reassurance.

'Look, you go for coffee with your friends after school, right? What's the difference coming to mine? I'm your friend, aren't I?'

'It's not the same though, is it?'

Sebastian stepped off the pavement, tilting his head back slightly. 'It's not a problem; let's leave it for another time. Catch up soon, hey?' He began to check the road for traffic so he could cross.

'No, wait! I'll come with you . . .'

They began to walk along together, him filling the light summery air with questions as he tried to find out as much as he could about her. She answered his queries amiably and without suspicion, even though she still seemed slightly shy around him, nervous almost.

'I don't really remember much about your house but I know I stayed here when I was younger,' she said slightly meekly.

'No . . . no, well, I don't suppose you would . . .' He was distracted as he put the key in the door.

'It's where you and mum were brought up, isn't it?'

'No.' Sebastian frowned, pushing the door back so that Caroline could enter first. 'What made you think that?'

Caroline ran her hands along the piles of newspapers that now lined the walls through the hallway. 'Mum said.'

'This is where your grandmother lives but it's not where we were brought up.'

'What are these for?' Caroline opened a broadsheet from the top of one of the piles.

'They're archives, I collect them . . . for reference.'

'Oh. There's a lot.' She laughed.

And there *were* piles of them everywhere. A daily collection had accumulated rapidly into something monumental. They were all neatly stacked from floor to ceiling in most places, as though he was fashioning a new kind of wallpaper. The collection had grown even faster since Yvonne had gone to hospital, somehow signifying her absence.

Caroline stepped into the sitting room which was similarly lined with newspapers. She wandered tentatively around and it reminded him of Alice exploring the rooms down the rabbit hole. She suddenly looked really tiny. He watched her frowning at all the broadsheets: stacks of them making their way towards the entrance like giant paper buildings. Her hand moved to her throat and he waited for her to comment further but she didn't. Old familiar feelings from the past resurfaced and he could feel the draught rising in his stomach again. He needed to regain order, she was formulating a judgement and he hadn't been given time to make her understand, to see it from a different perspective. He walked across the sitting room to a small table in the corner and began straightening some correspondence he had laid there.

Looking up he caught her smiling at him – not in jest or repulsion but a real smile. He felt the draught subside and it was quickly replaced with an overwhelming urge to make her happy.

'Come and look at this!' he grabbed her hand and pulled her into the passageway, leading her up the steep staircase.

When they reached the top floor, he opened the door to a large and impressive room. All the walls had intricate Victorian cornicing visible which had a fresh coat of white paint, and even the floorboards had been sanded and glossed. Just recently he'd hung some deep teal coloured, taffeta curtains above the large windows and they were stark against everything else, drawing the colours from his portraits. He'd made a lot of changes in the room since he'd moved in; his art now filled almost two large walls. In one half of the room he'd placed two long white, leather sofas so you could view his work from all angles. In the middle was a rectangular glass coffee table held up by a carved granite sculpture. An ostentatious crystal chandelier hung directly from the centre of the ceiling. All items he'd picked up from junk yards and restored. It was all too much for the tall terraced house but he knew it was mesmerising nonetheless. He'd finished it over a week ago and he still loved it when he walked in, reminding him of art galleries he'd seen, where he pictured his work being displayed in the not too distant future. It was pristine, not an ornament or book in sight. The contrast from the dusty darkness downstairs to upstairs made them both blink – it was so clean and bright. Caroline was speechless. She was so shocked that she hadn't even noticed her fingers were still loosely entwined in his, reminding him of days with Cecelia. He pulled his hand from Caroline's, the balance not the same.

'Look,' Sebastian said as he grabbed her arms and turned her towards the main wall.

Caroline followed his gaze to the largest portrait behind the door, his latest work. It was a painting of Cecelia, but it was covered in blotches of oil paints in so many colours that only Sebastian would know what it was.

'Who is it?' The uncertainty in Caroline's voice was clear.

He hesitated, unable to hide his surprise that she could decipher a face.

'You can see it's a person?' He watched her for a few moments, willing her to recognise the familiarity.

'Of course I can see it's a person.' Caroline tipped her head to one side until she was almost bent over.

'Male or female?' He gestured to the painting with his hands.

Caroline stared for a moment at the vibrantly domineering picture.

'Female, I think . . .'

Sebastian toyed with the idea of telling her who it was but decided against it. She'd lost the thread of the picture and he didn't think she'd understand.

'It's a woman crouching.' She tried again, wanting to impress him. 'Is she naked?'

'Look at these.' Sebastian pointed to the linen etchings, distracting her from the picture, wanting to keep the mystery of who it was to himself. Caroline was beautifully intriguing, but she wasn't Cecelia and he was feeling the loss of his sister more keenly than ever before.

'I love that smell.' Caroline lifted her head, breathing in the atmosphere filled with turpentine and oils.

Sebastian smiled, leading her over to his most recent artwork. Ava's eager participation had meant his rooms were filling up quite rapidly.

'How did you do this? Who is it?'

'It's a technique I started using when I was studying for my A levels. I find something I want to etch, cover it in linen and use a mixture of charcoal and powdered paint to project the image onto the cloth. It's a friend of mine.'

'Are they all parts of the body?' Caroline was tipping her head again, making Sebastian want to straighten her frame.

'They are, yes. Although some are clearer than others. The shoulder blades didn't have the right result. I think I'll just stick to hands and feet. Maybe faces.'

'Have you tried doing anyone's face?'

'Yes, they're all in the other room. I'm trying to keep them separate, so I can build up a portfolio of faces.'

'You can try it on me if you like? I don't mind. Why are they all parts of the body?'

'Because that's what I'm most interested in.' Sebastian examined her face, the exaggerated features she'd inherited from Cecelia.

'So, do you want to?' Caroline said, piercing his thoughts.

'Do I want to do what?' He reached into his back pocket and removed the tobacco pouch where he had some cigarettes.

Caroline snatched one from his hand, looking at him defiantly while she waited for him to get his lighter out. She was trying to impress him, assert herself, see how far the boundaries were set. He was intrigued to see where she would stretch it to.

'This.' She waved her hand at the linen etchings pinned to his easel. 'You said you're experimenting with faces so I'm offering you mine.'

Sebastian shook his head and moved across the room to sit on one of the sofas.

He placed his elbows on his knees, head in his hands and breathed deeply. The line was cast and Caroline was reaching the shore.

'Are you all right? Have I said something wrong?' Caroline followed his steps and tentatively sat next to him.

After a few moments he looked up at her, tears glistening in his eyes. He was waiting for her to tell him about Lydia, a sign she trusted him, but he needed her to feel some sort of empathy towards him. Hesitantly, and with practiced steadiness he lightly placed his hand on her knee. His thumb pressed into the small hollow fold of her bent leg.

He could feel the draught rising up again like a gentle swirl of smoke from a newly lit camp fire and he had to suppress the almost overwhelming urge to touch the other leg because he knew it would be too much for her at this time. All he wanted to do was check the symmetry, see if it was the same.

'I'm fine. Come on, your mum will be worried about you. You should go.'

'I've upset you, haven't I?'

Sebastian held her gaze. 'Not at all, Caroline. I'm just finding it hard to adjust . . . and things aren't good right now with Mum being in hospital . . . I miss her . . . I miss your mum as well actually. I thought things would be different when I came out . . . that she'd forgiven me. I guess I just have to be patient.' He looked up and smiled softly, going along with the lie Cecelia had possibly told Caroline.

The sudden change in his demeanour would worry Caroline, he knew that, cause her curiosity to stir and swell. And he was right, it had. The atmosphere had changed and beneath the miasma an entire, intangible mist was swirling around their feet and he wanted to grab her hand and dive in. It was enough, he'd done enough.

He stood up, a signal for her to leave. 'Come and visit me again soon.' He embraced her briefly, squeezing her shoulders, his fingers touching the line of the sharp pointed blades, the draught subsiding, somewhat.

'She'll come round. I'll speak to Dad and he'll talk to her.'

'I'm fine, honestly,' he said, smiling as he placed his hands in his pockets.

She got up from the sofa, hitched her school bag across her shoulder and walked ahead of him out of the room and down the stairs. He watched the shape of her calves, the slight jolted movement of her muscles through her tight white jeans as she walked. The symmetry, the perfect symmetry.

They reached the front door. 'If you're serious about becoming my muse, pop round again in a couple of days.'

'OK, I will. Thanks for . . . well, thanks.'

'Bye,' he called, as he watched her walk down the street.

Back inside he wandered around Yvonne's living area feeling completely lost. Spending time with Caroline had reminded him of the hours he'd spent in his cell recalling the moments he'd sat in the bath drawing Cecelia's beautiful frame. His imagination had shown him memories so clear that he'd been able to feel the hot water on his legs, the steam covering his nose, the faint taste of newly smoked tobacco in his mouth and Cecelia's laughter, her quiet chatter. And now he couldn't recall any of these memories with anywhere near as much clarity.

The problem Sebastian was battling with was that he didn't feel symmetrical; in fact, he'd felt completely off balance since being released from prison. The confines of the stark building had kept everything tied up in a neat package and now he'd been spat from the large security gates, the string had come undone. He'd lost his extra limbs, the matching side to his own form. His sister.

Sebastian still, even all these years on, reached out in the night for Cecelia, like an amputee who can feel their missing limb. It cut the words from his mouth, the breath from his lungs, leaving him lonelier than he'd ever felt in his life.

Sitting down in Yvonne's living room he took himself back to the first night of his release, so he could possibly try to erase any thought processes detrimental to him now, because he'd sat for hours, contemplating his future, pondering his suicide.

Then he'd realised, quite shockingly, that he wasn't prepared to go anywhere without Cecelia. Death could easily take his hand and lead him away but he wasn't going to accept the invitation without her.

That night the moment had passed and Sebastian had felt as though he'd stepped onto the other side of death, his ego gently coaxing him from the edge of the bridge, the frayed rope, the kicking away of the chair. But now, he felt different. Now he felt happy to die alone. He sat in the chair as the dark turned into light and another day began to unfurl.

16

The soft sound and the pattern of the footfall told Cecelia that Samuel was coming down the cellar stairs. She didn't stop what she was doing or turn to see what he wanted. This was where they were at the moment; how their relationship had developed. In the strained, exhausted tone that had become his voice since he'd decided to change his role from husband to carer, he spoke.

'Your brother is at the door.'

She paused briefly. 'Tell him I don't want to see him.'

'Is that it?'

The emphasis in the sentence echoed but she chose to ignore it. 'That's what I said.'

She heard the more purposeful steps as he turned to go back upstairs. She stopped what she was doing and placed the freshly cut pictures on the table. The cellar was her domain, the place she came when she needed time to think, to meditate, as she had done since she'd lived there. She was continuing with her project. She would cut out sentences from old books, words she liked, and stick them to the walls to make a collage. On and on it went – she wouldn't settle until she'd finished the entire room. The books she used usually appeared in junk shops sold as job lots; occasionally they were delivered to her through her business and had missing pages or spines so they were unwanted, unsellable. Not to her though; she loved these more than the fully formed, perfect ones she sold in her shop. She would spend hours cutting out sentences and paragraphs, illustrations of knights and damsels, beautiful flowers and fantastical sea creatures.

Idly and without much thought to the pieces of paper, she moved them around the table. She felt strangely tranquil, like she'd been drowning and had suddenly released the fight. Floating back to the surface, breathing again. Even the arrival of Sebastian hadn't really disturbed her.

Heavier, more serious footfall broke her thoughts. She hitched herself onto the table to give her feet a rest and saw Samuel appear, a sombre look draped across his face.

'Cecelia, you need to come upstairs and speak to Sebastian.'

She breathed deeply. 'Can you not just do one thing for me, Samuel? I don't want to talk to him. Please ask him to leave.' She stared at him over her glasses.

'Your mum's dead.'

Holding his gaze for a few moments she suddenly became aware she wasn't breathing. Steadily she took in some air.

'Can you please tell Sebastian I have nothing to say?' Pushing herself off the table, she continued to trim the new pictures she'd laid out.

Samuel moved towards her and she flinched as she felt his arms around her body, holding her up, always ready to fix everything.

'Come on love, you need to speak to him.'

Shrugging him off she turned to face him. 'You haven't let him in? Where's Caroline?'

'Did you hear what I just said?'

'Yvonne's dead, I heard you the first time.' She pushed past him and made her way upstairs to the kitchen, up three more steps to the sitting room where she was astonished to see Caroline talking to Sebastian.

'Caroline, please would you go to your room and finish your homework.' Her heart pounding, she prayed her daughter wouldn't argue for once.

Watching Caroline's face darken, she matched it with a look of her own. Eventually Caroline got up, said goodbye to Sebastian and went up to her room.

'Bye, Caroline.' Sebastian stared at Cecelia as he said it.

She folded her arms defiantly. 'You really are a piece of work, aren't you? You've been asked to leave, now go.'

'Have I? News to me.'

'We have even less to connect us now and certainly nothing to discuss. I'll leave the funeral up to you, I won't be coming.'

'I don't know where all this hostility has come from, Cecelia. Whatever you think of Yvonne, she's still our mother . . .' His voice broke and he leant forward, resting his head in his hands.

She turned to see Samuel and Caroline standing in the doorway, slight looks of shock on their faces.

'I told you to get upstairs, now do as I ask.'

Caroline tutted and folded her arms. 'I'm not a child!' She stomped off up the stairs.

'I know what you're doing, Sebastian, don't think I don't. Now get out of my house or I'll call the police.'

'Cecelia!' Samuel shouted, disappointment clear in his voice.

'Stay out of this, Samuel. It wasn't long ago you would have thrown him out yourself. Didn't you say that when he was released from prison? Since you had a nice little chat with him, you've changed your mind. Pathetic.' Cecelia knew she sounded childish but she was feeling singled out, alone amongst her own family.

She felt Samuel's hands on her arms, restraining her emotions again, shushing her as he always did, trying to fix things she didn't want him to.

'You're in shock, just sit down a minute and listen to what Sebastian has to say.'

Cecelia flung her arms free. 'Fuck off with your bedside manner; I'm not one of your clients!'

'I'm just trying to help.'

'Well, don't.' She turned to Sebastian. 'I'm asking you calmly, to please leave my house. You're on licence, you wouldn't want me calling the police.'

To her surprise, Sebastian stood up, raised his hands as if in defeat. 'OK, I'll go.'

'You'll find your own way out. You know where the door is.'

She turned to watch him leave the room and then her attention was drawn to Samuel's astonished face.

'You really are a callous bitch at times.'

'I'll tell you what's callous, shall I? The fact that if I told you what he's really like and what he's been doing since he came out of prison, you wouldn't believe me. If you had any respect for me, you'd trust what I say and support me. When I say I don't want him here that should be enough. But no, because I'm forgetting, aren't I? I'm forgetting that you think I'm mad, or was it crazy as I heard you say to your mother the other day? Because everything's my fault, isn't it? Our daughter dying was my fault!' Cecelia was becoming hysterical and she knew he was even less likely to listen to her if she began screaming.

She watched him walk away – heavy and tired – into the kitchen. His silence was enough. His lack of argument told her that she was right – he did think she was to blame.

She had an urge to follow him and confront the situation, but something told her to leave it. There were things she didn't need to hear or say. She began counting to calm herself down: one . . . two . . . three . . . four . . . the cold breeze inside her began to subside as she thought about where she'd put her tablets.

It was in this quiet moment that she heard the front door open. Spinning round she saw the back of Sebastian just as he closed the door behind him again. She sank down into the chair nearest to her as she felt the miasma descend like a heavy mist around her.

17

The draught descended when Sebastian realised it was Cecelia standing at the front door instead of Ava. He wasn't in the mood for Ava this evening. Since he'd taken an interest in her life the other evening in the bath, she'd become far more intense, assuming an understanding of him, when she actually knew very little. When he'd asked her not to call round for a few days, she'd become very defensive about all the artwork she'd enabled him to do, as though she had some sort of ownership over it. All he'd asked her for was some time to himself, but her reaction made him see that this wasn't a relationship he needed right now.

Sebastian nodded his head at Cecelia.

Even though he didn't particularly want her to come into the house, which he now felt was his domain, he offered anyway, knowing she would decline. As she talked he could see her eyes wandering past him and into the house. Reflections of memories flitted across her face and it pleased him. She was remembering and that was all that mattered to him.

'I don't want Caroline coming round here. If she turns up, tell her to go home ... and stop waiting for her outside the school ... it's weird.'

'OK.' He shrugged and went to close the door but to his surprise Cecelia caught it with her hand.

'Let me put it another way, so you understand. If I find out you've spoken to her or seen her, then I will call the police.'

'Spoken to or seen who?'

He smirked as he watched Cecelia take an exasperated breath.

'Caroline.'

'Oh yes. Caroline. Pretty girl. Very intelligent. Well, I should be grateful.'

'What for?'

'Last time we spoke you were going to kill me and now it's just a call to the police.'

'Just stay away from us, Sebastian.'

'I can't stop her coming round, Cecelia. And calling the police would be pointless. I believe she turned seventeen a few months ago?'

He watched Cecelia staring at the ground, struggling to get a grip on the situation. He knew her so well, a fact that she'd clearly forgotten since he'd been in prison. They were one and the same and always would be.

'Why is it so wrong for her to see her family? I *am* her uncle.'

'Because you're filling her head with lies.'

'I don't know what you're talking about, Cecelia. You're the one telling all the lies. If she asks me a question I'll tell her the truth. You learn that in prison.' He lowered his voice as an old woman laden with shopping bags slowed as she passed, trying to hear what was being said.

'Evening!' Sebastian called. She muttered something back and quickly moved on, embarrassed he'd drawn attention to her. His hand hovered in mid-wave and then gently he lowered it to his mouth, resting his fingers on his lips. He talked over Cecelia's head as though someone was behind her.

'It would be terrible for her to learn that you lied about who killed her grandfather.' He squinted as though he was thinking. 'I'm not sure how that would affect your relationship with her.'

He looked down into her matching eyes, the dark forest of her irises, daring her to challenge him, contradict what he had said.

'Well, I can't stand on the doorstep chatting all evening.' He stepped back and slammed the door in her face.

He knew that now she would go home and do some real damage with her daughter. Telling a teenager not to do something would inevitably make her want to do it even more, especially when Samuel was on his side. He'd had quite a conversation with Samuel at the hospital before Yvonne had died. Obviously feeling vulnerable, he'd confided in Sebastian about everything that had happened since Lydia's death and the state of Cecelia's fragile mind.

Rummaging through an old box of records he'd found in his mother's cupboard under the stairs, Sebastian searched frantically for the record she used to play when they lived at the farm. He hadn't known what made him think of it but he suddenly had an overwhelming desire to hear it again. He eventually found it: Schubert – Ständchen, Cecelia's favourite. Memories of their time in the loft room, a time when they'd been happy, rushed in, giving him the same feeling he'd had then when it was just him and his twin.

Less than two hours later, Sebastian answered his door to a sobbing Caroline.

'I'm not supposed to let you in.'

'OK, I'll go.' She looked as though he'd struck her and the draught rose inside him.

His immediate reaction was to grab her as she turned away but he stopped himself. The last thing he wanted was the eyes of the inhabitants of the other houses on the road witnessing him dragging a young girl inside.

'Come in,' he called to her. She stopped and slowly turned back.

In the hallway she stepped into his embrace, as he kicked the door closed with his foot. He gently held her, breathing in the scent of her hair, the same smell as Cecelia's. After a few moments he kissed the top of her head, patted her back and led her into the sitting room.

'What's all this about, hey?'

'Mum told me I can't come and see you anymore but she won't give me a proper reason why. Ever since Yvonne died she's been acting really weird. I know it's a big thing losing your mum, but she didn't even like her. We were never allowed to see her and she was supposed to be my grandmother.' Caroline tried to take a breath and he watched her vulnerability deepen on the intake.

'Death does affect people in different ways, perhaps she just needs some time.' He walked over to the table in search of his cigarettes.

'But what I don't understand is why she hated her so much. Why she hates you?' She lifted her hand towards him.

Flinching, he reached up to the mantelpiece for his lighter. 'Did she say that?'

'Well . . . not to me but I heard her and Dad arguing about you the other night. I'd be able to accept it better if she explained it to me properly.' She pulled at the bobbles on her lacy scarf. 'Anyway, I'm seventeen so I can do what I like.'

Sebastian pulled some tobacco from his lip and wiped it on his jeans. A warm mist was filling his chest, lifting the corners of his mouth, as he recalled Cecelia at Caroline's age. She had been adamant that she was grown up, but her behaviour suggested otherwise.

'That is quite true, but there are certain things that aren't acceptable for you to do, and whilst you live with your parents you really have to abide by their rules.' The hint hanging in the air that if she lived with him things would be different was subtle, but he watched it land favourably in her lap.

'Will you explain to me what's happened between you and Mum?'

He laughed. 'I would if I knew the answer to that myself.' He sat down at the table. 'Perhaps it's because I've been to prison, maybe she thinks I'll be a bad influence on you, I don't know.' He shrugged.

Caroline nodded but he could see she wasn't satisfied.

'You must remember I was sentenced for murder, Caroline.' He gave her a very serious look causing her to blush. 'It's OK, I can talk about it. It's not a secret.'

'I know. But I don't like to bring it up and embarrass you. I read about it on the internet because Mum said she didn't want to discuss it.'

'Well, that's understandable, don't you think?'

'Yes, but you were protecting her. Wasn't he abusive? She should be grateful.'

'Caroline, I was sentenced for killing a man. Not just any man. My father.'

She nodded again and looked at the floor.

'Can you see why that would make your mother wary of me being around you?'

'But she knows you, knows you're not a bad person. Even Dad doesn't think I should stay away from you.'

'Oh?'

'No, I heard him saying to Mum that she should give you another chance because you were only protecting her. And everyone deserves a second chance.'

'That's very noble of him.'

'But you were very young and it was self-defence, from what I understand. Your father tried to attack her and you came in at the right time.'

Clearly, Cecelia hadn't told her the full story. She had denied they'd been fighting and Sebastian had received a heavier sentence because he'd killed his father over a fictitious attack. Only Cecelia knew her reasoning behind this but he had his suspicions. Anyone knowing the truth would begin to ask questions. And he knew Cecelia didn't want anyone knowing the truth, especially not Caroline. It was easier for him to continue carrying the blame because he didn't have any children.

'Yes, but even so . . . only the people present at the time know what happened . . .'

'But the truth came out because you went to prison, you were punished . . . I don't know. I don't know what to think anymore, especially with all this stuff she's telling Dad about Roger and her mum. That's not true, is it?'

Sebastian stood up, placed his cigarette in his mouth and held out his hand for Caroline to take. The draught was turning cold, rising within him and he needed it to subside.

'Come upstairs with me.'

Caroline was reluctant at first and he realised the slight sharpness in his voice had alarmed her.

'Come on, I'm not going to hurt you, I just want to show you something.'

She relented and allowed him to pull her from the sofa. Up the two flights of stairs they went and into the sparse white bedroom where his art work was accumulating rapidly. When he wasn't on the market stall he spent all his spare time painting, experimenting with new techniques.

'Sit down over there.' Sebastian pointed to the sofa directly opposite the picture.

'You've shown me this before.'

'I know, but you clearly didn't take it in the first time.' He put his arm around her shoulders and pointed to the painting.

'Do you think she really believes it?'

'Who believes what?' Caroline's voice was small, lost in the large white room.

Sebastian tutted and squeezed her harder, pulling her into his enthusiasm for his masterpiece. 'Do you think your mother believes what she's saying about her parents?'

'I don't know ... I, I don't know what you're asking me. Is that her? Is that a picture of my Mum?'

Sebastian stood up and walked towards the portrait and then turned to look at her.

'Yes, it is. But you don't know what to say, you don't know what I'm asking you because you're too young. Or what you think I want to hear. But I don't want you to do that, Caroline. I want you to think for yourself. Your life is still in black and white but it'll change, the grey areas creep in as you grow older.' He sat back down next to her, making sure he was on the opposite side of her this time, so he could reach his arm around her again and feel the curve of her other shoulder.

'All you need to do is have faith. Have faith in your gut feeling, what rises in your stomach when you're near people, when they speak to you, because that holds all the answers. It leads the way for us all.' Caroline glanced at him nervously. He gave her a symmetrical squeeze and smiled, trying to lift the atmosphere.

'Stop looking so worried.'

'Are you one of those religious nuts? You know, because you've been to prison and all that.'

A deep laugh escaped his lips and he got up to pace around the room, switching the stereo on as he passed it, playing the vinyl he found earlier, filling the room with Cecelia's favourite song.

'No, not at all! Look, I learnt a lot of things in prison. I spent hours studying and reading and even when I was lonely, I always knew what was right and wrong for me. Because that's different for everyone.' He got up from his seat and walked over to the portrait, gently running his fingers over the ridges of paint. 'It's not religion, Caroline, it's reality, and it's my belief that came from what I learnt. Every time I read some kind of philosophy, I thought about your mum, my twin sister – she is my religion, if you like. She's everywhere I look, even when we're apart.'

It was pleasing to him when she also got up from her seat and began to properly look at the portrait. It signalled to him that she was listening, beginning to see art as he wanted her to see it.

'I know it sounds weird but sometimes it feels like Mum has really lost herself . . . sometimes I think it's because you've been apart for so many years . . .'

'I've always thought that twins are one whole. We started off as one, then became two and then one again. It doesn't matter how far apart you are physically.'

'Yes! I hadn't looked at it like that but yes, that's exactly how it feels. Mum has always said something like that.'

Sebastian shook his head. 'It comforts me to know your mum has said that Cece. I wonder sometimes if we'll ever be close again, if we'll ever get over what happened.'

She frowned. 'Why did you call me Cece?'

'Did I?' He sat down on the opposite sofa.

'It doesn't matter, it just sounded odd.'

'You remind me so much of her. Of your mother.' His voice had become quiet and low and he was descending with it. 'Can I ask you something?'

Caroline nodded, her fingers still touching the portrait.

'Who is Lydia? I've heard her mentioned a few times . . .'

'Lydia?' Caroline's face had taken on a look of astonishment, then tears filled her eyes. 'She was my twin sister. Mum must have told you about her?'

Sebastian wanted her to tell him about Lydia, even though he knew some of the story. 'No. I haven't really had any proper conversations with your mum. I overheard a few things about Lydia, mainly from Yvonne.'

Caroline's face crumpled in pain, blowing the draught up within him. 'Lydia was knocked down outside the school and died. Mum was driving.'

18

Yet again, Cecelia felt the heavy hopelessness fall around her like an elevator stopping mid-floor. Having had to deal with Sebastian several times since Yvonne's death, it occurred to her that she'd been affected by it all far more than she'd first thought. Her brother was matter of fact about the whole situation and insisted on calling to try and involve her in the funeral decisions. She had said she wasn't interested in being involved but that wasn't true, she just didn't know how to deal with the unresolved tension between them. It made her realise she had been punishing Yvonne for years with her silences and absence; shutting her out of her life, not allowing her to know her grandchildren. She had never once given any thought to the fact she might actually die.

Cecelia had gained immense satisfaction whenever Yvonne had tried to contact her, and the pain she could cause. Now Yvonne was gone and Cecelia realised that maybe there were things she had wanted to say to her mother, needed to tell her. But now it was too late and Cecelia was surprised by how sad she was about it. The last time she'd seen Yvonne was when she'd visited her in hospital, not believing she was as ill as everyone had been saying. Not wanting to believe it, needing someone to hate. Cecelia was almost jealous of Sebastian for allowing Yvonne into his life.

Reflecting on her childhood didn't even help to justify why Cecelia kept Yvonne on the outside of her staged existence. It was too late now though, she kept telling herself. Too late to change it all. Now she had to think about what she was going to do with White Horse Farm. She would need to involve Sebastian, something she didn't want to do. And other more pressing matters drifted into her mind: her ever unsynchronised marriage, the complicated relationship she had with Caroline, Yvonne's funeral. This was the first hurdle she had to get over. Somehow, through much manipulation, Sebastian had convinced Samuel to conduct the procedure. The arguments had ricocheted around the walls of her sanctuary that day, trapped and desperate to escape, like a dozy house fly. Another subject to disagree on, how could they possibly not. She showed adversity with everything he suggested and vice versa, as though they knew their roles had to be contrary to one another, their descriptions within their marriage.

Because she had lost this argument, Cecelia now had to deal with the fact that Yvonne's body lay in a coffin in the funeral parlour that was in the grounds of their home. Their own garden was fenced in but there was a long drive leading down the side of their property, the land at the bottom having been used as a builder's yard by the previous owner. This had now become the main funeral parlour, after Samuel had decided his father's old premises hadn't been big enough for him to offer a high quality standard of service. The old place was now used merely as a shop front to advertise the business and greet families.

Samuel had suggested Cecelia visit Yvonne in the chapel of rest, but she'd refused vehemently. She didn't see any point in seeing the empty corpse of the woman who had done nothing for her when she was alive.

And now she had to contend with Sebastian's arrival at two o'clock that afternoon to check that Yvonne was correctly positioned in her coffin and to say his own private goodbye before the actual service the following day. Samuel had empathised with him like he did with all his clients and it had irritated Cecelia like a burning skin rash.

The manipulation was blowing in the breeze like an old uninhabited cobweb but Samuel couldn't see it. The more she tried to point it out, the further away she pushed her husband. But as long as Sebastian stayed away from Caroline and she from him, that was all that mattered to her. All she could think about now was getting rid of Sebastian before Caroline came home from school.

Elements of her daughter were clearly a part of Sebastian's make up and this connection was something that worried Cecelia. Every day, Caroline did something that reminded Cecelia of Sebastian. It was half-day closing and she'd managed to shut the shop at lunch time and return to the cool comfort of her cellar, clearing her head, calming her nerves.

Familiar laughter coming from the direction of the garden told her someone was heading towards the house. She looked up through the tiny window that gave a small view of the embankment leading up the garden. There she saw three pairs of feet. Samuel's, Caroline's and a pair she didn't immediately recognise. Sebastian's.

Running up the cellar stairs and through the kitchen she met the three of them just as they were coming through the back door.

'What are you doing out of school so early?'

Caroline tutted. 'I told you I had free periods for study this afternoon, you must have forgotten. I did come to the shop but you'd already left.'

'It was quiet and a half day so I closed. I've been home a while, but I didn't hear you come in.' She put her hands on her hips, watching Caroline intently, slightly out of breath and desperately trying to ignore the stares of her brother and husband.

Her daughter rolled her eyes and she tried to swallow her irritation. She didn't want Sebastian to see they weren't getting on.

'Strange you two should turn up together, or is that just a coincidence?'

'No. I bumped into Sebastian outside the café opposite the bookshop. You weren't around so he took me for lunch.'

'Oh did he? Well, you should be studying, so go and get a few hours in before dinner.' She stared at her defiant daughter, dared her to question her. 'Now.'

'Just a minute.' She pulled Caroline back by her arm. 'Have you been drinking?'

'No!' Caroline shrugged herself free.

Cecelia leant in to smell her breath but she couldn't detect anything. There was definitely something different about her demeanour though. A something she didn't like.

Making sure Caroline went all the way up the stairs and satisfied she'd heard her bedroom door close, Cecelia turned to face the room. Sebastian had already pulled out a chair at her kitchen table and Samuel was fiddling around with the kettle, not wanting to get involved.

'Right.' Cecelia took a deep breath. 'Sebastian, I have reluctantly allowed you to coerce Samuel into arranging Yvonne's funeral. I've also had to accept you coming here for the arrangements. That's about as much as I can take. Please do not shoehorn yourself into my family. We discussed this the other day and nothing's changed.'

Unnervingly he held her gaze, completely absent of any humiliation at her request. She nodded her head for him to respond or leave but he stayed exactly where he was.

'Mum, you're being unfair!'

Cecelia turned to see Caroline at the bottom of the stairs. 'Please go back to your room and get on with your revision. This has nothing to do with you.'

'But –'

'Just do it, Caroline! For once in your life, do as I say.' She moved towards her as if she might strike out and a pain rose inside her as she saw Caroline flinch before she ran back upstairs shouting about how much she hated her.

Cecelia took a few deep breaths before she turned back round to face Sebastian. As she expected, he was smiling, not obviously but enough for her to notice.

'I understand you want to try and fit in somewhere, belong to something. I get it. But it's not here, not with my family.'

'Cecelia . . .' Samuel turned from his coffee making, a look of dismay on his face.

She nodded – he was disappointed in her. That would go nicely with the other disappointments she'd provided him with just lately. She knew he was fearful of shouting, instead choosing to speak to her as though she was a child. He wouldn't want to tip the scales of her delicate state, using a passive aggressive alternative to get his point across.

Cecelia pasted on a false smile. 'Sweetheart, would you mind leaving us for a while please? I need a private word with Sebastian.'

To her utter amazement, he did exactly what she asked.

'I'll go and check on Caroline.'

Cecelia leant on the back of the chair opposite Sebastian; his eyes hadn't left hers through the whole conversation with Samuel.

'Please, Sebastian. I need you to stay away from us. After tomorrow there will be no reason for you to see any of us again. That includes Caroline.' She observed him taking in what she was saying. His mouth always made the slightest of movements when he was in contemplation, almost a pout, and his eyes would take on the merest of squints, but still he was silent.

'I know it must be difficult, all that time in prison . . . but you haven't come out with nothing . . . you've got half of White

Horse Farm and Yvonne has given you a roof over your head, and there'll be more to come after the funeral . . .' She was floundering, his constant stare and presence unnerving her. 'Go and make something of your life. Do all the things you planned to do before . . . well before, you know . . .'

He looked at her pointedly, his eyebrows rising slightly.

Just as she began rambling again, he got up from his chair and moved around the table towards her. She flinched but her pride and stubbornness wouldn't allow her to move and she was beginning to wish she hadn't been so hasty in asking Samuel to leave.

Sebastian reached forward and touched her cheek with his thumb and then did the same with his left, allowing his hands to linger around her face. She leant backwards, holding her breath. Then his hands carefully spread around her jaw and he pulled her head sharply towards his face.

'You'll never get rid of me, Cece; I am a constant in your life. You so easily forget that we are one and the same. I am you, you are me.' Then he leant over and whispered in her ear. 'Give my best to Lydia . . . Tell her I'll catch her next time.'

All she remembered after that was the slamming of the front door as he left.

19

Caroline was a good liar. Sebastian had been surprised at how quickly and easily the false words had slipped from her mouth. As he left Cecelia's house, he reflected on the precious few hours they'd just had together over lunch.

They hadn't bumped into each other at all, as she'd said, but instead she'd called round for him. He'd just finished experimenting on Ava with a new art technique and it had turned out better than he'd expected, making him warm to her again. She'd given him the space he'd needed and hadn't called round for some time, drawing him towards her instead of the other way round. He found he'd missed her company and was pleased to have rekindled their relationship, using the excuse that he'd been upset about Yvonne, which was, in part, the truth.

Answering the door in only his jeans, he'd been breathless. Ava had still been upstairs getting showered and dressed – activities he often liked to watch. Since he'd started using her as one of his muses her body had become more graceful to him and she seemed taller and more confident.

'Oh. Have I disturbed you?' Caroline looked concerned.

'Not at all! Come in, come in!' Sebastian grabbed his T-shirt from the back of a chair and pulled it over his head.

'Let's go upstairs, I'll show you what I've just done.'

Caroline followed him, caught up in his excitement. 'What is it? You're covered in blue paint!'

'Do you remember I told you about Yves Klein the other day? How he imprinted naked women on linen using paints?'

'Yes . . .'

'I've tried it out on a friend of mine and it's turned out better than expected. Come and see.'

Sebastian opened one of the bedroom doors at the top of the stairs revealing a floor covered in large pieces of linen with blue smudges all over them, the ghost of anatomical parts imprinted, some clearer than others.

Caroline just stared at his work, dropping her school bag onto the floor.

'What's wrong, don't you like it?' Sebastian watched the disappointment on her face.

'You were going to experiment on me. Why didn't you wait?' Tears sprung to Caroline's eyes.

Sebastian grabbed the tops of her arms, startling her somewhat. 'Oh, Caroline, you're too young for all this. And what do you think people would say if they knew I was using my naked niece as a subject? It would be a bit weird.'

Caroline shrugged, reminding him again of Cecelia at that age.

'Look, I'll tell you what. How about I do some work with your face and hands using the linen? I could take some pencil sketches of you too if you like?'

'OK...'

'Caroline, believe me when I say, if you weren't my niece I'd gladly use you as a subject. But I can't, you must understand that?'

A naked Ava walked up the stairs from the bedroom. 'I can't get this blasted paint out of my hair ... oh sorry, I didn't realise you had company.'

'This is my niece, Caroline.'

'Oh, hi Caroline. I've heard so much about you – quite the favourite niece,' she said, smiling and rubbing her hair with the towel, making no attempt to cover herself, which embarrassed Caroline.

'It's not difficult, the other niece is dead.' Caroline smiled sarcastically, jealousy clear on her face.

Sebastian and Ava both laughed at her comment, taking it as a joke.

'Your uncle said you make him laugh.' Ava reached forward, running her fingers down one side of Caroline's long hair, making her lean away slightly. 'Pretty girl ... Sebastian, I'm going to get dressed and make a move, I've got stacks of work to do.'

'OK, beautiful, see you later.' Sebastian pushed past Caroline and kissed Ava.

'Don't go on my account.' There was a hint of irritation in Caroline's voice.

'No. I really need to get back.' Ava wrapped the towel around herself. 'I'm sure I'll see you another time. It was nice to finally meet you.'

'And you.' Caroline couldn't hide the juvenile jealousy in her voice and it made Sebastian smile.

Perfect. There was more than one good use for Ava after all, apart from the obvious. She'd just let Caroline know he'd been talking about her.

'I could cook you dinner later, Sebastian, if you're around?'

'Yes, that would be nice.'

An awkward silence began to drip down the walls and seep into the room as Ava went off to get dressed, Caroline's dislike of her clearly apparent.

Sebastian grabbed Caroline again. 'I'll tell you what, why don't I make you some lunch? Open a bottle of wine?'

'Only if you have time . . .' Caroline continued to sulk.

'Well, I have to do something to put a smile back on that face. Can you imagine what my linen artwork would look like with a miserable mush like that? The paint would go off.'

They both began to laugh, the atmosphere lifting immediately. They were like children – just as he and Cecelia had once been.

Yet again, Sebastian whisked Caroline up in his enthusiasm and she followed him down the stairs to the kitchen. Two glasses and a bottle of white wine sat on the table. He opened the wine and poured them both a drink, handing a glass to Caroline. She took it tentatively.

'Have you got school this afternoon?'

'No. I have study periods for the rest of the day.'

Sebastian nodded, sipping his wine. Clearly she wasn't going to study.

'Why don't I have a quick bath and then we'll go out for lunch if you like?'

'Great . . .'

'What's wrong?'

'Nothing.' She said it as though there was a question mark.

'Come on. Say what you need to say.'

Caroline sipped some more wine and stared up at him.

'If I needed to, would you let me live here?'

'What, with me?' Sebastian tried to look surprised.

'Yes . . . only if things got really bad at home.'

'Yes, of course you could. You'll always have a place here with me.' He smiled; his day was just getting better and better.

'Thanks . . .'

'Come on, finish your drink and let me draw you.'

'What?' Caroline's eyes widened, her cheeks flushed pink.

'When your mother and I were younger, I used to sit in the bath and draw her.'

'What, naked?' Caroline pulled a face; the wine was seeping into her veins and making her relax.

'No! Just her head and shoulders.' He swigged his wine, hiding his lie. 'You have a beautiful symmetry about your face. Let me, just for half an hour before lunch.' He was trying to make up for her earlier disappointment.

Caroline stared at the floor for a few moments. He could see she wanted to but didn't know if she should. She was at that age where she was caught between the standards her parents had set and wanting to make her own decisions.

'And here's the girl who just got in a strop because I wouldn't let her get naked and writhe around in paint and linen.'

'I wasn't actually going to do that . . . I was just feeling a bit jealous of your friend, I suppose.'

'An artist is never faithful when it comes to his muses.' He smiled at her. 'You know you're my favourite girl, right? Now then, are you going to let me draw your beautiful face?'

Caroline smiled back. 'OK. But you get in the bath first and shout me when you're ready. I don't want to see . . . you know?' she nodded at him. 'That would be weird!'

'Very weird indeed.'

Sebastian smiled at this wonderful memory now. Only a few hours had passed since he'd shared the moment he'd waited so long to have with Caroline. The wine had helped her to relax and he'd managed to draw some intricate pencil sketches of her face.

And now, Cecelia had nudged her daughter even closer towards him. He walked home via the churchyard in search of his niece's grave; Lydia, who he would never know, because Cecelia had been careless with her little mice and allowed one of them to die.

20

Cecelia woke to find herself halfway along the track that ran down the side of her home, leading to the funeral parlour. Initially she was disoriented; she had thought she was already awake. Lydia had been leading her somewhere again and in her mind it had been every bit as vivid as reality – the cold air on her skin, her breath in the night sky, plumes reaching up to the stars. She looked down at her hand, expecting to see a smaller version of her own, but it was empty.

Instead of walking back to the house and getting into bed, she continued along the track, wincing at the small shards of stone pricking the soles of her bare feet. Her teeth chattered fitfully – the summer evenings were coming to an end. The quarter moon shone its blue light, showing the edges of larger objects, but the rest were muffled in the darkness. The security light flicked on as she approached the building, blinding her for a few seconds.

I have to see her, she told herself. It's the only way to heal. Her determination was keeping her warm in only a cotton slip.

Pausing, she turned to look around for her little girl, but she'd gone – lost in her own world of sleep, slipping in and out of her dreams.

Upon reaching the wooden-clad building she was surprised to find the door unlocked and she could see a light on in the back room. Heart thudding, she moved forwards tentatively. Her first thought was that it must be Samuel. His insomnia would often take him by the hand and lead him to his work; a forgotten detail, a new idea that wouldn't wait until the morning.

Tiptoeing through the rooms, stumbling across a chair, she made her way out to the back. She should have been frightened, nervous, but so many years around Samuel's work had removed the creepiness surrounding the cadavers that had passed through the back door. It was their stories that made them seem sad and macabre; they wore them like death tags on their toes. But Yvonne had a different story and it was her who Cecelia had come to see before she travelled with her on her last journey.

The room was empty apart from the rows of coffins. Tired and distracted, Samuel must have left the light on and the door unlocked after the long day.

Yvonne lay on the main table, lit up like a shrine, the light bouncing off the brass handles of her casket. Cecelia stayed where she was, frozen to the spot; the top of Yvonne's face was visible like a white wall mask. Stepping forward, Cecelia peered in, intrigued to see what Sebastian had chosen for her to wear. It was trivial but important to her nonetheless. She had an impression of Yvonne in her head, of a woman who had deserted her children, had chosen her own needs over theirs, and Cecelia didn't want to see a reformed version, a softer, kinder face. When she'd heard about Yvonne's heart attack, she'd begun to imagine her as a frail old woman, a victim. But then she'd seen her in hospital and she hadn't looked that bad, nothing like Cecelia had expected anyway.

Leaning into the casket she stared at the face of this stranger who had played a part in bringing her into the world.

'Why did you stop visiting me?'

Cecelia almost choked as she took in a sharp breath and turned around to see Sebastian standing behind her.

'What the hell are you doing here?' She stood with her back to the coffin, hands gripping the edges of the table.

'Answer my question, Cece, and I'll answer yours.'

'No. Get out!' She looked past him and through the window, hoping that Samuel would notice that she was missing and come down to the funeral parlour.

'Just answer that one question and I'll leave you alone.'

'What? Like I owe you something? I didn't ask you to kill anyone for me.'

'You really do believe your own lie, don't you? I didn't kill anyone, remember?'

His voice was becoming deeper, darker and she desperately wanted to be on the other side of the door.

'Look Sebastian, we're very different people and . . .' She was trying to stay calm and not get angry with him.

'Are we, Cecelia? Are we really?'

'What's that supposed to mean?' She couldn't help snapping back.

'The thing that scares you the most is that you know what you are and what you are capable of. And you know that I never would have done what you did. I had so many chances to kill Roger but I didn't. You're the murderer, not me.'

They stared at one another, their identical eyes boring into each other.

'You're capable of just as much as me. Why did you have to serve another three years on top of your sentence?'

He took a deep breath. 'He was a nonce, Cecelia, and I was provoked . . . What does that matter now anyway?'

She couldn't help laughing at the false irony she'd fabricated.

'I'll tell you why I stopped visiting, shall I? Because I wanted to make a life for myself. I didn't want to be forever reminded of the past. If you remember, you refused to see me on that last visit.'

'You gave up on coming because I didn't turn up for one visit?'

'We're not twins. Not in the true sense of the word. When we're together, you make up three parts of us. I'm that tiny quarter smothered by you.' She glanced at the reflection that the tiny shard of crescent moon cast on the window. That was how she felt within their relationship, a fragment.

'Look up there.' She pointed to it, desperate for him to understand. But when she looked back, he was gone and she was standing there alone.

She spun around and around, searching for him.

'What are you doing?' A harsh whisper startled her. It was Samuel.

'I was . . . I . . . just . . . I was sleepwalking . . . I must have been sleepwalking.'

'Why are you covered in mud?'

'What?' She looked down at her grey slip. It was smeared with soil and dirt, as were her hands and knees. 'I don't –'

'Oh my God, Cecelia, have you finally gone completely mad?!' He was looking past her and she followed his gaze to Yvonne's coffin. Protruding from her mother's chest was the knife Cecelia had hidden on the window sill. It rose proudly from Yvonne's body.

'It wasn't me! I didn't do that!' Cecelia peered uncertainly down at her hands. 'It was Sebastian. He was here a second ago . . . I promise you, Samuel.'

The look he gave her was a mixture of pity and anger and she knew no amount of talking would convince him she was telling the truth. They'd been here before and the increase in her sleep-walking of late would only convince him she was getting worse instead of better.

'Come on, sweetheart, let's get you back in the house.'

'No, Samuel, I promise you it wasn't me!' She felt like she was a child again, being led away by Roger whilst desperately trying to protest her innocence. But the more she struggled and rambled, the madder she sounded. She'd lost the battle – this was the end of her reality and the beginning of another terrible dream.

21

Sebastian had realised that watching someone without them realising was easy – no one ever seemed to notice him doing it. It was an activity he hadn't had much opportunity to do during his time in prison. But having spent many hours reading psychology textbooks, he'd learnt to get a more rounded view of himself and other people, and the idea of who he could be within his own scenery.

Casually he wandered down the alleyway and went through the back door of his house, not wanting to be seen or heard going through the front at this late hour.

In the kitchen he washed the engraved knife he'd removed from Yvonne after Samuel had led Cecelia away. Tiredness suddenly swept over him, but he didn't want to sleep, the latest events with Cecelia still playing through his head. Instead, he made himself a pot of tea and stoked up the fire, the summer evenings having turned autumnal, a chill in the air.

The café opposite Cecelia's bookshop was the ideal place to hide in the shadows. It was old-fashioned, dark and dingy – Cecelia thought of it as a mild threat to her own business where Sebastian knew she wished people would stay and drink the coffee she offered whilst deciding which books to buy. It was clever, he granted her that. If people had a hot drink, they felt obliged to make a purchase. But it was the perfect place for Sebastian to sit and watch Cecelia and Caroline.

He'd observed Cecelia's day-to-day life in the shop: her rituals, her foibles, her busy times, quiet periods. The regular intake of medication, the hours Caroline worked for her, the fragile relationship they had, the strong love Cecelia had for her daughter, which was so easily dismissed by Caroline. He'd watched all of this through the large grey looking glass of the shop windows. Then at night, he watched them through the lit windows in their home. Why so many people lived in such an exposed way baffled him. When he longed for the dark he could close his shutters and say goodbye to the world for a few hours.

At Cecelia and Samuel's house there were always lights being turned on and off in the middle of the night and on that one particular occasion he'd witnessed Cecelia sleepwalking late at night when he was leaving a bar where he'd met Ava, as he did on most evenings. It had been like looking through the windows of a doll's house and he felt like a giant. He'd got a glimpse into Cecelia's life – everything she didn't want him to know.

A banging at the back door startled him from the darkness. He picked up the engraved knife before he went to see who it was. For a brief moment he thought it might be his probation officer or the police because he hadn't been sticking to his curfew, but his instinct was telling him it was Caroline.

'I don't know what to do!' Caroline cried, as soon as he opened the door. She ran straight into his arms whereupon he wrapped her up like a doll, kissed the top of her head and told her everything would be OK.

'Come. Sit down and tell me what's happened. Does your mum know you're here?'

'No . . . no, she's gone mad. I told Dad I was leaving, I can't take it anymore . . . What are you doing with that?'

Sebastian looked across at the blade on the table. 'I took it away before your mother hurt someone with it . . .'

Caroline nodded, completely taken in by his story, not thinking to ask him when he'd removed it.

'Give me your mobile.' He grabbed it from her hand before she'd answered.

'What are you doing? No, you can't ring them.'

'I'm going to speak to your dad and just let him know you're safe here with me for tonight.'

Caroline reluctantly gave in.

After he'd reassured Samuel, made tentative enquiries and told him he'd bring her back in the morning, he sat down with Caroline. The deep glow from the fire in the dark room lit up her beautiful face and, for a moment, it took his breath away.

'You're up late.' She sniffed through her tears.

'Night owl, always have been.'

Caroline nodded, tears beginning to streak her face.

'What's wrong, beautiful?'

'It's my grandmother's funeral tomorrow and I didn't even know her. I feel sad about that.'

Sebastian clenched his jaw and started rolling himself a cigarette.

'You need to understand that your mother is ill . . . she always has been . . .' He took a deep breath, feeling the draught lift. 'A bit highly strung.'

'Is that why you don't get on anymore? Mum keeps telling me you're both very different people.'

'We're not different at all. Underneath it all, we're the same. Where she's highly strung, I have accentuated emotions in another area. I wouldn't call that different; I just pour my passions into my art. We think and feel the same, it's just that sometimes your mum likes to convince herself she's an individual . . . and she's not. It's not possible to be when you're a twin . . . you know that.' He offered her a cigarette.

'Yes . . . yes, I do. I miss her terribly. No one understands, they just say that time will heal and I'll come to terms with it. But I won't. I don't think I'll ever feel the same again. I don't think I want to.' Caroline tapped her forefinger on the table and Sebastian noticed her shift in her chair and lay the cigarette she was holding down on the table and repeat the action with the other hand – an obsession with symmetry that they shared.

'How long have you been doing that?' He nodded to her hands.

'What?' She quickly pulled them from the table, hiding her embarrassment.

'I just watched you tap both hands on the table.'

She sipped the tea he'd poured and he could see she was wondering whether to confide in him or not.

'I've always done it . . . more so when I'm anxious. Lydia was the same.'

'Me too. It must run in the family.'

'Really?!'

He nodded. Caroline's eyes lit up, the beautiful green eyes he so desperately wanted to draw as he had done only earlier that day.

'Do you have to do everything twice, so it's equal? Like when you scratch, say . . . your ear, you have to do the other one?'

'Yes! And then sometimes again with the opposite hands.'

'Ah, a kindred spirit.' Sebastian lit his cigarette.

'Does it really run in the family? Me and Lydia thought it was normal until we realised our friends didn't do it.'

He laughed. 'You don't want to be like everyone else, do you, Caroline?'

'No.' She looked down at her lap.

'Come on, time for bed. We've got a long day tomorrow.'

'Thanks for letting me stay. Where am I going to sleep?'

'You can have my bed and I'll sleep on a sofa in one of the other rooms.' He could have slept in Yvonne's bed but that felt strange to him so soon after her death and he wanted to be as close to Caroline as he possibly could.

'Oh, no, I couldn't do that.'

'It's clean, if that's what you're worried about.'

'No! I just don't want to throw you out of your bed, that's all.'

'Conceited little thing, aren't you? I often sleep in other rooms of the house, sometimes down here in the chair. Us creatives don't need much rest.' He reached across to the desk drawer behind him, rummaging for his sleeping tablets.

'Here, take one of these, it'll help you sleep.'

Caroline hesitated. He could see she was still unsure whether she could trust him, balancing on the tight rope of Cecelia's opinions.

'I'm not going to poison you. The doctor gives them to me for my insomnia.' The contradiction in what he'd just said was lost on her. 'They'll calm you and give you a good night's rest. You'll feel better, I promise.'

Caroline took one and drank it down with her tea.

'Keep it to yourself though. I shouldn't share my prescriptions with anyone.'

She nodded at him and he held her gaze for a brief moment. Flashes of times with Cecelia scorched through his mind, memories of when they'd been children and just like Caroline and Lydia.

'Right, come on, I'll show you where to go. Do you want one of my T-shirts to sleep in?'

'Oh . . . yes please, I didn't bring anything with me.'

Sebastian checked his watch. Caroline would be asleep in approximately fifteen minutes.

Once she was in bed, he sat with her, holding her hand, offering her comfort in the dead man's hour. This was the time Sebastian enjoyed the most – when he could feel the stillness and the full force of the low ebb. A strange period during the night, where the frail didn't survive and the insomniacs couldn't relax, he would allow himself to slip beneath the miasma and watch Caroline as she slept, becoming his sea horse, his beautiful, symmetrical other.

22

Freshly showered, Cecelia sat in the garden room, a cold cup of tea welded to her hands, she'd held it for so long. Even the hot water hadn't warmed her perished skin and as well as looking pale, she felt it too, a diluted version of her original self.

Through the long glass door, she could see Samuel in the distance under the pergola, resurrecting their daughter's grave. She uncurled her hands from the cup and placed it down on the coffee table. The noise seemed to be far louder than necessary and she flinched. Examining her hands now, she tried desperately to remember digging at the grave, but nothing came to mind. In her head were only images of Sebastian and Yvonne, but her hands were scratched and sore and her fingernails still held remnants of mud. Picking at them so hard she made them bleed and at one point she thought she'd lift the nails off, so desperate was she to erase the traces.

The decision to have Lydia buried in the garden had been solely hers – Samuel had been too grief stricken to give much input. She had to be close to her, know she was near her in the garden.

There was a circular patch of flowers in the spot where Lydia had liked to sit cross-legged, reading a book. For some reason, daisies had always grown there spontaneously and Cecelia had told Lydia that it was because they liked the special little girl who sat there. But one day Cecelia had come home from work to find Samuel filling up a large swimming pool he'd had delivered, covering the beautiful grass where the daisies had grown. Once the girls had grown bored with the pool and Cecelia had convinced Samuel to dismantle and sell the damn thing, the grass had rejuvenated, but the flowers had never grown back. After Lydia had died, Cecelia had dug out a circular patch and planted all types of daisies on it, imagining Lydia sitting there as she always had done, lost in a story.

Samuel had added a bench as a memorial, an idea Cecelia had found abhorrent at the time. But now, it mostly offered her great comfort, except today.

The high-sided blue pool loomed in her memory. There had always been too many children in there. Too many legs and arms flailing around, little people squealing – she'd been constantly petrified something would happen to one of them. How ironic it was that she'd never thought of losing her daughter in the way she had done.

It was her fault. She knew that. She'd been unable to explain to the rest of her family what had happened that day outside the school, the shock temporarily erasing her voice. When it did return, she repeated the events over and over again, as if saying it out loud would reverse what had happened. They'd promised one another they'd always watch their precious girls, never take their eyes off them, make sure they were safe at all times. And yet, through all this worry, Cecelia had managed to kill one of them.

And still, all these years on she couldn't bear to talk of Lydia in the past tense. Everyone had said to keep her memory alive and that's exactly what Cecelia was doing. She continued to talk of Caroline and Lydia as she'd always done, watching her grow in her imagination as Caroline was doing in reality. She'd even altered her bedroom in accordance with her age. But her little spirit pulled her back, constantly haunted her, looking exactly the same as she had that day, undeveloped since her ninth birthday. The memory of her lying in the road was constantly there, picture perfect in her mind; hitting the bonnet, the ground, the sound of the brakes screeching. Lydia was pulling her back, wanting Cecelia to see her as she was when she left. Cecelia realised that now. And she could also see how Caroline had suffered, Samuel too, but she'd been blanketed in her own grief, selfishly wrapping herself in its shroud.

Parents had stopped their children coming to play at Cecelia's house and they hardly ever had visitors. Cecelia had thought at first that it was because they were embarrassed, lost for words. Then she realised they were frightened, scared their own children would meet a nasty fate. You can't go to the undertaker's house – they're cursed, it's a dangerous place. All sorts of cruel words bounced around her house at that time. That Cecelia had been drinking, that she hadn't been paying attention to the road, talking on her phone. None of these rumours had been true; she just hadn't seen her daughter run out in front of her. She didn't even register it was her until she stepped out of the car.

Cecelia had been caught up in these cruel words as though she was entangled in a large fishing net, so much so that she couldn't see, hadn't seen that there was another little sea horse sinking towards the sand at the bottom of the ocean.

23

It was the knocking at the front door that stirred Sebastian from the chair where he was sleeping lightly. He hadn't left Caroline's side and had watched her sleeping for most of the night.

Running down the steep staircase in just his shorts, he wrenched the door open to Ava. He didn't want to see her and the draught reached his throat before he could control it.

'It's not a good day to call.' He pushed the door to close it but her hand stopped his efforts.

'I know what day it is – you told me last night, remember? I wanted you to have these.' She handed him a bunch of cream roses. 'You went out late last night, everything OK?'

'Just fancied a walk, I needed to clear my head.'

The draught was accelerating and a vision of her hanging from a noose, a wooden chair lying on its side beneath her slowly swaying body clouded his vision. It wasn't beyond his grasp to make the image reality.

'Look Ava, I like you a lot but I don't need someone question-ing my movements every minute of the day.'

She held up her hand to silence him.

'Please don't. I understand, you don't need to explain, I get it … I wasn't checking up on you, I was concerned, that's all.

You're right, it is none of my business what you do. I was just trying to be a friend.'

Sebastian nodded and closed the door. He just wanted her to leave him alone today. When she showed concern, it irritated him. He knew that was why relationships went wrong, when one felt they had a claim over the other. He wanted her to accept what they had instead of trying to push things all the time, sending them back to the start. He needed to concentrate on Caroline for the time being. His beautiful, symmetrical, utterly perfect Caroline.

Laying the flowers on the table in the sitting room, he made a pot of tea and took two cups up to the bedroom; he wanted to be there when Caroline woke up.

Unfortunately, Ava had ruined that moment for him because she was already awake.

Leaning over her, he straightened her ruffled hair and then kissed her on each cheek; her eyes were squinting, heavy with sleep, showing two slithers of green crystal.

'I feel dreadful, not sure sleeping tablets agree with me.'

'Takes a while to get used to them and your body probably needs more rest. You slept well though.'

He sat down in the chair as she tried to pull herself up in the bed.

'Did you stay there all night?'

'Yes. I wanted to make sure you were all right.'

'Thanks.' Caroline reached for the tea cup he'd placed on the small table beside her.

'Once you've had some breakfast, I'll take you back so you can get ready for the funeral.'

'I don't really want to go back.' Her voice was croaky, still cranking itself forward.

'Well, you don't have any clothes here, so you have to.'

'If I did have my stuff here, would you let me stay?'

Sebastian rested an elbow on each knee and clasped his hands together.

'Is it really that bad at home?' he asked, already knowing the answer.

Caroline clasped her tea cup even harder and blew on the steaming hot drink. He could watch her for hours, every movement she made, like a never-ending film. All the years he'd missed with Cecelia were rushing up to greet him now that he was with Caroline.

'It's never been OK really. I used to think it all went wrong after Lydia died but now, when I look back, I can see things weren't right way before then. Mum was always preoccupied; do you know what I mean?'

He nodded, lifting the heels of his feet onto the chair, wrapping his arms around his legs, childlike, as he always did when there was any talk of Cecelia.

'Sounds exactly like my mother . . .'

'She's always called that house her sanctuary, but it was more like a prison. We weren't allowed to go out anywhere – not to friends' houses, the park, anything like that. We had to stay in the garden and friends had to come to us.'

'Why?'

'Because she was frightened something would happen to us. She was always taking us to the doctors as well, demanding we have tests, although I've never worked out why. I used to think it was normal until I realised my friends weren't up the doctor's every five minutes. Madness, when you think about what happened to Lydia . . . her involvement in it.'

'I guess some of that is to do with everything that happened.'

'I can see that now she's told me. But we didn't know any of it at the time. Didn't know we had an uncle or another set of grandparents – we didn't think to ask. I didn't even know what happened to her mother until she told me about you . . . I kind of remember her from when I was younger when we stayed here for a bit, but she never told us who Yvonne was.'

'Do you know why you came to stay here back then?'

'Mum and Dad needed a break from one another, that's all I know. They've never really got on, not that I remember anyway. We were pleased to have Eleanor, Dad's mum, with us.'

'I don't think a relationship with anyone was ever going to work for Cecelia.'

'What do you mean?' Caroline frowned, causing Sebastian to reach forward and iron out the crevices with his thumb.

'Don't spoil your beautiful face.' He relaxed back in the chair, crossing his legs. There was no need to throw her any bait, he already had her. 'Your mum never really talked about Roger's death, didn't seem to grieve over him. I think it affected her much more than she let on and she couldn't really interact properly with anyone except me afterwards.'

'She hated him, didn't she? Roger, I mean. And Yvonne left too – it must have been hard.'

'I think your mum was convinced Yvonne would take us with her and when she didn't, well . . . she couldn't cope with it. The truth that she'd left her behind was too much to bear.'

Caroline raised her head as if in agreement.

'To be honest, I don't take too much notice of what she says . . . Mum hasn't been able to work out what's real and what's imaginary for quite some time.'

Sebastian held his breath, willing her to go on, but she just stared into her cup.

'It must have been really difficult after Lydia died?'

Tears became visible on the rims of her eyes and he felt the draught stirring, a desire to hold her so tightly she might stop breathing gripped him, but he stayed where he was.

'I went to live with Eleanor, in her side of the house for a while – Dad was struggling with Lydia's death, and he and Mum just weren't getting on. It affected Mum badly. She ended up on heavy medication and I didn't go back to stay with them for over three years. Sounds silly because it was only the other side of the house but it felt like I was somewhere completely different. I think that's why Mum and I don't get on now.' She put her cup down on the bedside table, breathing out deeply, as though she was cooling her face, causing her fringe to flicker as she desperately tried to hold back the tears. 'She was like a stranger to me and we never got our relationship back. It was like going to stay with a foster parent . . . not that I know what that's like but I can imagine. It was just weird . . . all weird . . . we had to pretend Lydia was still alive, like it had never happened.'

'In what way?'

'Oh, you know, making birthday cakes for her, decorating her room when mine was changed . . . that kind of thing.' She sighed. 'Have you got anything I can take? I feel dreadful.'

Sebastian looked at her enquiringly.

'Something to pick me up?'

Sebastian breathed in deeply through his nose and turned to look out of the window, giving himself time to think.

'I've done it before.'

'Done what before?'

'You know . . . a line.' A small smile lifted her symmetrical lips. 'Come on Uncle Sebastian, I know you do it, I've seen inside that box you have on the table in your bedroom. I looked when you were running your bath yesterday.'

'It's one thing me doing it, quite another for you.'

'I won't tell anyone. Come on, it'll make me better. I can't go to my grandmother's funeral feeling like this. It's probably just what you need as well.' She stretched her arms above her head and leant one way, then the other.

He stared at her for a long time, overcome and mesmerised by the movement, his overwhelming love for her warming even deeper in his chest.

'Go on . . .' She reached out and touched his arm.

'You promise me –'

'Anything!' she beamed.

'Let me finish. You promise that afterwards you'll let me draw you again?'

She frowned. 'Of course. I let you do it yesterday, didn't I?'

'I know, but I don't want you to think I'm being weird. It probably sounds like a strange thing to like doing, but it's not, not really. It wasn't to me and your mum anyway. I miss that . . . I miss her . . .'

'That's enough of that, Uncle Sebastian. It is my job to keep your spirits lifted today and if drawing me while you sit in the bath makes you happy, then that is what we will do.' She theatrically finished her tea and placed the cup back on its saucer. 'More bubble bath today though please.'

They both laughed and Sebastian stood up, waving his hands in a royal gesture before holding them out for her to take.

'I am my most creative when I am in the bath tub, darling!'

Caroline giggled, grabbed his hands and allowed him to pull her from his bed; enticing her towards him, further and further, deeper and deeper, into the mire.

24

After the funeral, Cecelia packed some of her clothes in a suitcase. Caroline had made it clear she wasn't coming home for the time being and wouldn't be persuaded otherwise. Samuel, clearly tired from it all, had failed to support Cecelia in her protests. Even when Cecelia had told him all the strange things Sebastian had done when they were younger in a desperate, pathetic attempt to see if that would make a difference. His response hadn't really surprised her – he was always so amiable about everything; showing a brief moment of shock and then subservience as he realised leaving well alone would be easier.

Just before Cecelia had begun to pack her things, he'd told her their marriage was over. But to her, it had never really started. It had been an escape route, a way out of her dismal situation. She had been seventeen and pregnant when they married. No prospects and no family interested in helping her. Samuel had promised to accept what he thought were his responsibilities, offering her a new life since he had been totally besotted with her from the very first time they'd met. But she had made every year they'd been together miserable for him.

Now that it was finally at an end, she told herself it was the beginning of something new. There were questions she'd carried around in a tiny suitcase she'd had as a child, and now she needed some answers.

Standing on a chair in her bedroom, she reached into the dark shelf at the top of the wardrobe, her hand straining for the handle; she'd shoved it right to the back, forgotten about it for all those years.

Stepping down hard off the chair, she placed the tiny suitcase inside the larger one she'd been packing and opened the lid. Leaning forward she sniffed the musty, cold smell that reached her nostrils – it hadn't been opened for so long. Violet sweets, wood from a sharpened pencil and the strong smell of notepaper hit her nostrils. She picked up the little case and sat down on the edge of her bed. There at the bottom lay her mother's letter, still unopened, the one she'd thought Roger had written. She opened it and read the words, 'I forgive you, love always, Mum'. Had she read it all those years ago, she'd have known her mother was still alive, that her father had been telling the truth. Keeping it safe was her soapstone hippo, the snout finally having dropped off. She closed the lid, placed it back in her suitcase and made her way downstairs, where she found Samuel sat at the kitchen table.

'Before I go, I've got something to tell you.'

'I know.' He looked up at her, his face pale, drawn. It was the first time she'd realised how tired and haggard he looked, older than his years. Guilt rose up in her throat again, the old familiar feeling of blame slapping her round the face, threatening to strangle her.

'What do you mean by you know?' She couldn't help sounding defensive, however bad he looked.

Samuel sighed deeply. 'I've been waiting to see if you were going to come and tell me before you left. I think I've wanted you to tell me for most of our marriage . . . maybe it would have made a difference.'

Cecelia pulled out a chair and sat down opposite him.

'I know you shot your father.'

For a few moments she held her breath, swallowing the words that were jumbled in her throat.

'That was what you were going to tell me, wasn't it?'

She nodded. 'Partly. Did Sebastian tell you?'

Samuel laughed. 'No. I've known all along.'

'How?' Cecelia's voice had become meek, distant, as it always did when she was upset; the ghost of her past muteness hovering around in the background.

'You told me once when you were sleepwalking, Cecelia . . . I think I knew, deep down anyway. Knew you were trying to make a go of it with me, pretend everything was normal because you couldn't deal with the guilt of what you'd done. I didn't really take it in at the time, not until after the twins were born. I think I justified it because you and Sebastian were so badly abused.' He swept his hand across the table as he always did when he was talking about something serious. 'What I can't understand, Cecelia, is why you didn't tell the truth in court . . . if you'd told the police what had happened, they would have taken pity on your story, especially as you were a girl. You were just children, provoked by years of abuse and with no mother around. It would have been manslaughter; Sebastian wouldn't have gone to prison and neither would you probably. I've wondered all these years if you actually wanted him out of the way.'

Cecelia stared at the table, the lines of the wood, the knots and the cracks where words had been trapped for years, and she was suddenly transported back to the farmhouse.

'I felt suffocated by him, I thought he'd grow up to be like Roger and I'd never get away from him.'

'But Cecelia, an innocent man – your own twin brother – went to prison. I just don't understand.'

'You never have understood, Samuel.' Tears fell down her face, fading and smudging the words that lay on the table. 'Don't you think I've felt terrible about the lies I've told? What I did at the farm that night scared me. I did it without any thought . . . I just shot him . . . dead. What does that make me?'

'I have no idea. What *does* that make you, Cecelia?'

'There's something else I need to tell you . . .'

'The twins aren't mine. Don't you think I fucking know that!' He banged his fist on the table. 'They don't look anything like me . . .'

Cecelia flinched, shocked that he knew her far better than she'd ever realised.

An icy silence wisped through the kitchen as they both rested on the dusty words left unspoken for so many years.

'I thought you'd be disgusted with me if I told you the truth . . . can you see why I needed Sebastian out of my life?'

'I don't understand . . . I thought it was one of your college friends . . .'

Cecelia began to sob again; she'd hoped he'd know what she meant without her having to say it out loud.

'What ...' Samuel stood up, his chair falling away from his legs. 'You have got to be fucking joking.'

'I was ashamed,' she whispered.

'Ashamed! Bloody hell, Cecelia! Bloody hell!' Samuel ran his hands through his silver hair. It had been a deep auburn before Lydia had died and seemed to grey overnight as if he'd passed away with her. The dark hair Cecelia had so wanted her children to have, so she could believe they were his.

'You should have told me from the start . . . I loved you.'

'That's part of the reason I didn't tell you.' Cecelia wiped her face with her sleeve. 'I knew you'd accept it, be too kind to ever bring it up and I didn't want that. I didn't want anyone to think it was OK, because it's not.'

'Except, you left out the part about your brother raping you . . . shit, we need to go and get Caroline.'

'Sit down, Samuel.' Cecelia frowned, slightly baffled by what he'd just said.

'We have to go and get her . . . why didn't you tell me all this before, I would have stopped her going there.'

'Sit down!' Cecelia grabbed his arm. 'He didn't rape me, Samuel . . . I never said he raped me . . .'

Samuel stared at her, then at her hand clamped around his arm before he shrugged her away and sat back down at the table.

'What?'

Cecelia took a deep breath. 'I know . . . and I don't want to talk about how and why, it just happened . . . we were young and I know it was wrong but . . .'

'But what, Cecelia?'

'Look, I'm not going to sit here and blame Sebastian. It happened, I'm not proud of it, but it's none of your business.'

'You are unbelievable. The result of what you did was two children, two children that I brought up and who call me Dad. It is quite clearly my business!' He leant forward making her flinch.

He stood up and continued the search for his keys.

'Where are you going?'

'I'm going to get our daughter. Regardless of what you say happened, I do not want her staying with him.'

Cecelia stood up and grabbed hold of him again. He shrugged her away violently and for a few moments they fought one another.

'Listen to me! Samuel, just listen to me!' she screamed. 'I've been over and over this. The more we tell her she can't see him, the closer we'll push her to him. '

'If she won't come home, I'll call the police.'

'No you won't! She's seventeen; she can do what she wants.' Cecelia's voice was fading and heavy with fatigue – she desperately wanted the day to be over. 'There is absolutely nothing we can do but keep an eye on her and hope she sees him for what he is.'

She looked up at Samuel as he leant on the back of the chair, gripping the wood. He knew the twins weren't his and he'd loved her anyway. And probably still would have even if he'd known they were Sebastian's.

'Caroline's different from me. She's tougher, not so easily led. She thinks he's her uncle. I know her, Samuel – if we don't make any more fuss she'll get bored and come home. Trust me, it'll be OK.'

'If he touches her, I don't know what I'll do.'

'She won't let him do that.'

'But what if he . . . you know, gets violent with her.'

'He won't do that, he loves her. He never did that to me. Ironically, I'm ashamed to say that, but he didn't. And you have to remember the kind of upbringing we had, the special bond we had as twins . . . I'm not trying to justify it. I know it was wrong but we only ever had each other. Sebastian won't hurt her, I know he won't. I know him better than anyone . . .' The jumbled words tumbled from her mouth.

'Why have you spent all this time trying to keep him away then?'

'Jealousy, I suppose . . . Visit her, call her but whatever you do, don't tell her she can't see him. She's stubborn and we'll lose her altogether.'

'OK.' He nodded. 'I guess you know him better than anyone.'

'And I know her better than anyone. It makes me feel sick to say it but she's part of me and Sebastian. I am him and she is me . . .' She stood up and clumsily tried to embrace him. 'But she's your daughter, Samuel, and nothing can change that.'

He relaxed into her arms and she felt his head move in agreement.

'I need to go away for a while, sort some things out. And then, when I come back, we can see where we're at?'

Their arms fell from one another, breaking their embrace.

'Let's see . . .' He reached up and touched her cheek with his hand.

'Just promise me you'll leave well alone, Samuel.'

There was more meaning in those words than he could possibly understand at the moment. Cecelia knew that leaving everything as it was could quite possibly be the very thing that would bring their daughter home. There was no other option.

25

1 MONTH LATER

It had been two weeks since Caroline had died and Sebastian had told no one. Not his nosy, overbearing neighbour next door and not even Ava.

Samuel had called on several occasions, even turning up at the house, but Sebastian had managed to send him away with the excuse that Caroline didn't want to come to the phone or the door. Give her some space, I know it's hard but she'll come back if you respect her wishes, Sebastian had reassured him. Cecelia had been in contact less and was more accepting that her daughter was angry and needed space to calm down. It left him time to spend with Caroline, although he knew, even through the fog of his madness, that it was going to be short-lived.

Newspapers were crowding the rooms; he'd still collected them as normal, followed his usual routine. More than ever, the broadsheets offered great comfort; the insulation they gave him seemed to shut the world out further.

Instead of going out walking, he spent a lot of his time with Caroline and some of it with Ava so she wouldn't become suspicious. Ava knew something was wrong but assumed he was grieving for his mother, so she gave him plenty of space, tried not to crowd him too much. But he was grieving for his beautiful girl, who he lay wrapped around at night in his mother's bed. During the day he would carry her upstairs and lay her in his own bed, sobbing uncontrollably, begging her to wake up. Every time he left the room he expected to return to find her lips pink and smiling, her eyes sparkling again, as though time would magically resurrect her from the dead. She couldn't be dead. She wasn't dead. Without her, he was dead.

That terrible day had played out over and over in his mind, so much so, he'd find himself reaching out to touch her in his imaginary visions as though his mind was projecting the pictures on the wall.

They'd been laughing about her terrible knowledge of geography while she sat on the chair in the bathroom, him drawing her from his usual place. She was giggly on wine they'd drunk and the cocaine they'd taken and then she'd had one of his sleeping tablets to calm herself down. Eventually he'd fallen asleep in the chair during the dead man's hours and when he woke up she'd gone. He'd picked her up, held her like a rag doll, shaken her and given her mouth-to-mouth, but she was dead.

Each time he ventured downstairs, he would stop in the room where she'd slept and wrap himself in the sheets, covering himself in her smell, lying in the imprint her body had left.

At first, he'd tried to continue with the daily routine they'd come to know in the short time she'd stayed, laying her on linen sheets on the floor of his art room so he could draw her perfect form, but it wasn't the same and in the end he would carry her back to his bed and sit in the bath for hours crying.

Then the crying ceased and the panic subsided when he realised he still had his Caroline, that she was just in another dimension. That was when drawing her wasn't enough – the pictures he'd pasted all over the walls post mortem lacked depth and he needed them to hold more of her essence, her form, an imprint that would make him feel she was still real. In his dark, angry moments he covered her in blue paint and took imprints of her body, hanging the linen artwork on the walls, convinced this would revive her.

26

Dust filled the gaping hole and drifted across Cecelia's legs, eventually reaching her nose and throat. She quickly pulled her sweater up across her face and coughed into it, almost losing her balance. The purlin creaked from one weight being replaced with another.

Leaning forward with the window hook had been nerve-racking enough, but knocking the suitcase and watching it fall made her feel as though she was tumbling through the ceiling with it; a crash had thundered through and shaken the usually mute old farmhouse.

As the clouds of dirty white dust cleared, she began to see the damage that she had done to the ceiling. She'd been so sure she could hook the suitcase by its handle. Her immediate thought was of what Roger would say, but the familiar childhood fears soon left her when she realised he was dead.

Leaning forward she waited for the dust to settle as a new picture emerged through the large hole. It revealed a part of the open suitcase, and lots of items inside – all of the things that Yvonne had said were in there.

Cecelia squinted, trying to clear her eyes of the grit that had landed in them as she peered closer. She bobbed up and down like a cat watching its prey, trying desperately to get a better look, but the objects were lost amongst the thick dust and dirt covering them.

Swinging her legs and feet back onto the purlin, she carefully pulled herself round to face the opposite direction and edged her way back to the door she'd previously wrenched open with a claw hammer, a sick, nervous feeling burning her stomach. Dreams of the green suitcase on the purlin swirled around in her mind; memories of the case and the boarded-up door just after her mother had disappeared. All she wanted to do was find out if her mother had been telling the truth that day in hospital – it would give her a better understanding of her childhood. Now she was disappointed because she'd thought for all these years that Yvonne had been hiding something from her, when it seemed as though she hadn't.

Whilst staying at the farmhouse the last two weeks Cecelia's head had been flooded with the past crashing in like huge waves. She'd stayed there to try and clear her mind, to see if a different environment would help her mental state. Her home with Samuel was filled with memories of Lydia. Clearing and tidying the old farmhouse that she and Sebastian now owned was meant to give her time to reflect on her marriage and family, but her mind had felt so separate from her and kept wandering back to memories from the past when she'd lived there as a child.

Even her fitful sleep was bombarded with dreams of how her life had been under Roger's rule. Memories she hadn't understood as a child now became clear. She recalled, on many occasions, finding her mother in the morning lying in an empty bath, a towel to cover her and one folded up under her head. It was now obvious that was where she'd been made to sleep and, look-ing back, Cecelia could see that these occasions usually followed Cecelia's punishments.

Several times she'd arrived home from school to find her mother standing in one of the old hangars with bare feet and no coat to keep her warm – the hangars were still cold, even in the summer. It had been the punishment Cecelia hated the most and usually occurred when it was dark. She would stand in the pitch black and bitter cold with her eyes shut so tight that they ached. Staring into the darkness produced too many ghostly shapes which were triggered by the whispering voices that had been unmistakeably real, some so close to Cecelia's ear that she had imagined she could feel warm breath on her skin. She always heard men's voices and she imagined them to belong to the ghosts of RAF officers from World War Two. Roger had told her that's what the hangars had been used for, embellishing his stories with haunting tales of dead pilots.

Shakily, her feet found the floor as her phone beeped. She retrieved it from the back pocket of her jeans and read the text message. It was from Sebastian. He wanted her to go over there; he had something to tell her. A slight panic began to creep through her legs, travelling up to her chest. She tried to ring Caroline's phone but it was switched off.

Sebastian looked strange when she first arrived – he was covered in blue paint, hair dishevelled and he looked as though he hadn't showered for a while.

'What's all this about, I've heard about Caroline not going to school? They called and asked Samuel if she was OK. When

I texted her, she said she was dropping out, going to take art at the local college.'

Sebastian nodded, but apart from shakily lighting a cigarette, he said nothing. Something was very wrong and a sick feeling was beginning to rise in her throat.

'Is she here?'

'Yes. She's upstairs,' Sebastian said, a slight smile wavering on his lips.

'Sebastian, what's going on? You're frightening me.'

'Well, the long and the short of it, Cece,' he took a long drag on his cigarette, 'is that she's dead. Caroline is dead.'

Cecelia stared at him, she could almost see the minutes passing. 'What? She can't be . . .'

'She most definitely is. I couldn't believe it at first either. I've been waiting for her to wake up for the last few weeks.'

'Let me see my daughter you sick fuck.' Cecelia tried to push Sebastian out of the doorway leading to the stairs but he wouldn't let her pass.

'Look Cece, I think she killed herself. I found her one morning . . .' Sebastian's face crumpled and he began to sob violently. 'I didn't know what to do . . . I just didn't know what to do.'

Cecelia knew she needed to calm him down, get the facts straight. 'It's OK, just tell me exactly what happened.'

Sebastian held out his arms to embrace her. She moved towards him, unsure of what to do. She desperately needed to calm him down and call Samuel. Then she took a sharp breath as she felt a punch to her stomach.

27

THE END

This is the end. This is the end. That was all Cecelia could hear ringing in her head as she lay on the cold stone of Yvonne's kitchen floor. This is the end.

These were the last words she heard spoken before the knife was pushed into her stomach and up under her ribcage. She'd thought she was entering her brother's embrace, as she had so many times before, but it wasn't until she staggered backwards, her legs giving way, that she realised what had happened.

Sliding down the cupboard door, she eased herself towards the floor, putting her hand across the wound; blood seeped through her clothes, warm and slow. She heard the knife clatter to the floor and Sebastian's footsteps thundering up the stairs. Her eyes took in the engraving on the blade, the knife she'd had so many nightmares about. Her superstitious premonition had come true. Help, she needed help. She was gripped by panic, but shock seemed to have paralysed her body. After a few moments she tried to lift her bottom half very slightly in order to reach her mobile phone which was tucked into the back pocket of her jeans. She managed to wrench it free, wincing at the pain which was burning across her torso and pulsing in her neck, timing her demise. One . . . two . . . three . . . four . . . five . . .

The screen of her phone was cracked where she'd landed on it but she was relieved to see it still worked. She managed to get through to the emergency services and was desperately trying to keep it together enough to tell them where she was, but it was like one of those horrible dreams she'd often had where she couldn't make herself understood. The operator stayed on the phone, talking to her the whole time, reassuring her that everything would be OK, that they'd find her, someone would help her. Her voice drifted in and out of her hearing and the room felt like it was upside down. She reached out her hand to steady herself as everything seemed to tip over and then all was still again. The stove was next to her and she managed to reach up and pull the tea towels from where they were hanging from the oven door handle, covering the wound with them, pressing as hard as she could bear.

Her words were becoming incoherent and the operator sounded like she was fading away. Cecelia could see her at a desk on the phone in the middle of the ocean and she was drifting across the ripples of the water, becoming more and more distant, further and further away. Everything was drifting away from her. This is the end, she whispered to herself.

Then Sebastian was standing over her again. He snatched the sticky, blood-spattered phone from her hand, switched it off and threw it in the sink.

'We don't have much time.' He knelt down, pushing his arms underneath her, trying to pick her up and causing the pain to intensify and more blood to seep from the wound.

'Sebastian, please . . . ' she whispered.

'It's OK, Cecelia. Shush. I won't leave you again, I promise. I just had to get everything ready.'

Lifting her from the floor, he carried her through the sitting room, twisting, turning and manoeuvring around the piles of newspapers that were now taking over the downstairs. He paused briefly at the foot of the stairs so he could catch his breath. She tried pleading to him with her eyes, the little voice she had left, fading in and out. But his vision was focused on getting her up the two flights of stairs to the loft room.

A heavy stench of decay reached her nostrils and caused her to gag. It was a smell she'd noticed when she'd first arrived but it was far more pungent at the top of the house.

She winced as Sebastian leant forward and laid her on the floor on what looked like large reams of material, before leaving the room. Looking up, her vision slightly hazy, Cecelia could see some of the walls had been painted in oils. She gasped as her vision allowed her to take in the linen art work covering the rest of the walls and ceiling: blue paint everywhere, hands, feet, breasts, ribs and faces. The other side of the room was covered with sketch drawings of a woman she didn't recognise and then her eyes focused on the pictures of Caroline, her beautiful daughter. She tried to move but she was paralysed with fear and pain. Everything was drifting away from her.

Her surroundings tipped and swayed as she heard him come back in the room.

'Caroline. Where's Caroline?' A whisper was all she could manage, her mind desperately clinging on to what little consciousness she had left.

'She's gone, Cecelia. Lydia took her. Lydia came and collected her sister.'

She heard a click and a tap, the familiar noise of the stereo they had used for many years being switched on and she was transported back to when they'd lived in the farmhouse together. Schubert's Ständchen began to float towards her, around her, through her and over her, music evoking strange emotions she didn't wish to recall.

'Caroline . . .' She reached her arm out and pointed weakly to the linen portraits.

'My post corpus work – they're beautiful, aren't they? All this will be exhibited in a gallery when we're gone, Cece. A beautiful tribute to Caroline, don't you think? And to us, I suppose.' Sebastian climbed over her so he could move her onto her side and lay behind her, his body against her back; how they always used to sleep, twins cupped together.

'I need to tell you what I did to Mother . . .' she whispered, incoherently rambling, unable to take in what he'd just said about Caroline.

'Shush, Cecelia. Go to sleep, none of it matters anymore.' He was drowsy from all the pills he'd swallowed, his voice slurring with the movement of the room. 'We must go to sleep together. I'm here with you; we'll never be apart again.'

Cecelia could feel herself drifting further away, visions of Caroline and Lydia jumped around in her mind, memories of happier moments in their lives. She tried one last time to fight but she'd lost all her strength and she knew there was no time left.

Sebastian held her tighter, kissing the back of her neck as he placed his hand across her nose and mouth, stifling her for the last time.

'Night, night, Cece. I love you.'

They died there together on the linen. Cecelia and Sebastian's final portrait.

ACKNOWLEDGEMENTS

With much appreciation I would like to thank the following people:

My agents, Paul and Susan Feldstein for their constant support and invaluable professional knowledge of the literary world. Mark Smith, Joel Richardson, Rob Woolliams and everyone at Bonnier, Twenty7 and Zaffre for giving me this wonderful opportunity. A special thanks to my editor, Claire Johnson-Creek who worked tirelessly with me on this manuscript. Emily Burns, Carmen Jimenez, Georgia Mannering and everyone in marketing. The design team who produced such a wonderful cover. Molly Powell and everyone at Whitefox who worked on the copyedit. All the authors at Twenty7 who I've had the privilege of meeting, for their encouragement and kindness, especially Tanya Ravenswater, Lesley Richardson, Graham Minett and Ayisha Malik, thank you for all your wonderful emails and telephone chats! It's been great getting to know you all.

A huge thank you to Joyce and Doug Carter, my lovely parents, my sisters, Claire Carter and Joanne Newman, Sarah, Michael and the rest of the Burrows for all their love and support. In particular, my mother for reading everything with a red pen in her hand and to my mother-in-law, Carol who was immensely proud and would have loved this moment.

A special thanks to the following people: my dearest friend, Vicky Jackson for her constant belief, excitement and encouragement and for setting me on the literary path. To Catherine Stevens, Tina Payne, Nicki Plaice, Ryan Plaice and Paige Sieben for eagerly reading everything I've ever written and their unrelenting support. My husband's cousin, Dr. Nikki Frater for her genius art expertise. Michael Gibson for all the inspirational early morning walks and Costa coffees!

I would also like to thank Stacey Clark, Bev Langridge, Bianca Lewis, Angelina Nizzardi, Martin McMechan, Dawn Ancell, Elaine Dery and Rebecca Wright and her family.

My biggest thanks is to my husband, Christopher, for his constant, unwavering optimism and total belief in me. Thank you for the most exciting seventeen years.